Flights of Fancy

Flights of Fancy

Thirteen tortuous tales of science fiction, horror, bizarre events, and just plain weirdness

by

Harry Fancy

Spritsail Press
Williamsburg, Virginia USA

Flights of Fancy copyright © 2014 Harry Fancy

ISBN-13: 978-0-9825525-0-6
ISBN-10: 0982552505

First Edition 2014

Cover art by Brian Slack

Published by

Spritsail Press
Williamsburg, Virginia 23185

spritsailenterprises@gmail.com

Dedicated to harmless eccentrics everywhere.
Life would be so much duller without them...

Contents

Foreword

*F*lights of Fancy consists of thirteen quirky tales in an
equally quirky order, although the first happens to be the earliest.
"Archie's Room", which is a horror story, was originally drafted in 1961
but has subsequently been revised several times—as have most of my
pieces. I never know when to leave them alone—it's a bit like the urge
to scratch at a scab. Once they are in print I can no longer fiddle with
them, which is probably a good thing... Several of the tales—"Mirror
Image", "Train of Events", "Untitled Manuscript" and "The Private
Viewing"—can also be classed as horror stories. "The Private Viewing"
was actually based on a vivid dream I had when staging an exhibition
of paintings by an extremely talented and versatile artist friend of
mine, Brian Slack–who designed the cover of this book.

I am rarely excited by fantasy fiction which so often depends
upon magic swords or similar clichéd "cop-outs" but I do enjoy
classic science fiction and I hope that several of my offerings merit
being regarded as such. These include "Persistence of the Anima",
"Exclusive!", "New to Science", "Bandy and the Fort Knox Carpet",
and "Double Dealing."

"Exclusive!" is an oddity—it represents a page taken from
a magazine in which a communication from a gullible survivor of a
crashed space ship records what he has been fooled into believing is a
genuine translation of an alien recipe. The "continued on page 234" is
also a spoof—it follows a common but annoying practice in magazines,
of finishing an article on some remote page, where there happens to
be sufficient space. Don't bother looking for page 234—there isn't
one! Incidentally, "Bandy" seemed to write itself—I simply sat at the
computer and let my fingers dabble on the keys. (I hope that isn't too
obvious!)

"Take Two", "Manuscript Found on a Computer" and "The
Eternity Trap" are perhaps more quirky than most, being light-hearted
takes on religio-philosophical themes.

I hope you have as much enjoyment reading these "flights of fancy" as I did whilst writing them.

In fact, I hope you have twice as much enjoyment. Make that three times—I'm feeling generous!

Now, please, read on...

Harry Fancy,
Nether Kellet,
Lancashire, UK

Archie's Room

The old man cursed himself for a fool. How could he have done it?

His eyes strayed once more to the rough wooden crate. A pallid hand protruded stiffly from the sackcloth that was draped over the inert form. The tip of a patent-leather dancing-pump emerged from the other end.

At length the old man rose and, muttering to himself, drew back the covering. The face seemed to mock him; a handsome face with piercing black eyes and a neatly waxed moustache, which was twisted into precise, upward-curling ram's-horns. He was irresistibly reminded of one of those stylised illustrations of a leanly athletic Edwardian lifeguard—a former English half-mile cudgel-stroke champion, perhaps—about to demonstrate the method of applying artificial respiration. It was even worse than he had feared.

With a sigh, Jabez Gould, antique dealer, dropped the covering back over his latest, unwelcome acquisition. How could he have been such a fool? He kicked the box morosely, went back into the kitchen and lit the gas ring under an iron kettle. Whilst waiting for it to boil, he lit a cigarette and reflected, for the thousandth time, that his troubles stemmed from the by-pass. The two-mile stretch of fast, straight road had effectively cut off a small ox-bow of properties from the mainstream of life. Jim Thornton's garage had been the first to succumb, followed shortly afterwards by the "Green Parrot Cafe". The owners of the houses, on the other hand, were distinctly gratified by this increased seclusion now that virtually no traffic other than strictly local vehicles, found its way along the sinuous road which had once been so busy. So busy, and so perilous, with the ever-increasing volume of cars and lorries it had been compelled to carry until completion of the bypass some years ago.

The antique dealer no longer drove, his failing eyesight having made that impossible. Trade had atrophied, and the mountain had steadfastly refused to come to Mohammed in the lean shape of Jabez Gould. Several days could now go by without a solitary customer entering his cluttered shop. His best stock had been steadily bought up by more enterprising, more mobile dealers of a younger generation. They had waited for the inevitable lowering of his prices before snapping up his rather fine collection of snuff boxes, his Tunbridge-ware, the best of his porcelain, all the Mary Gregory glass, the firearms and edge-weapons. Some rather splendid musical instruments, most of the oil paintings and furniture had followed, leaving him with a motley collection of bric-a-brac.

Despite the vulture-like depredations, or paradoxically because of them, his stock had actually increased in volume in recent times, wily dealers having negotiated part-exchange deals for most of his treasures—a modest sum of cash together with a mixed batch of inferior goods being offered, and reluctantly accepted. These were offers he could not refuse; time and taxes for no man wait. The real antiques he genuinely loved had steadily disappeared in order that he might eat, however frugally.

This final folly had devastated him. A chance visit by a well-known dealer from the Midlands had coincided with a "final demand" from the electricity company. The gall of the man had been breath-taking. Smartly dressed in a pale grey suit, with a carnation in his button-hole, his slicked-down hair covering an incipient bald patch, he had strutted round the shop, pointedly brushing dust from his manicured fingertips as he poked and prodded at the residue of the old man's stock.

"Nothing really in my line, Mr. Gould. Let's see, now—you used to have some nice little Baxter prints at one time; still got 'em, eh?" Jabez shook his head sadly.

"Naw, don't suppose you have—not any more. Trade bad, is it?" Without waiting for a reply, he continued "Wish I could help you, but there's nothing here, really, is there?" He took another condescending glance around the shop. "Lor'—just look at that!" He pointed to a huge external horn gramophone which was visible in the shadowy kitchen beyond the shop and laughed without humour. "Bottom's dropped right out of the market for that sort of thing. Ten, twelve years ago you'd have got quite a packet for that. But not now. Left it too late. Missed your chance, old lad!" He allowed his hands to droop expressively.

Jabez, desperate for cash, almost begged him to take it, but the man was resolute. Nothing in the shop was worth his while; he turned to leave. Jabez implored him to wait, just for a moment. The man from the Midlands hugged himself as the old man started to ascend the dark stairs. He knew the old devil must still have something tucked away—he had a nose for it...

The old man entered his bedroom sadly and took a small box decorated with porcupine quills from a cupboard. He eased open the lid. Inside, on a bed of cotton wool, lay four exquisite netsuke—tiny carvings executed nearly two centuries ago by a Japanese master-craftsman. Three were of ivory, probably walrus tooth, and were miniature sculptures of birds, animals and foliage. The fourth, although simpler in form, was sensitively carved from a flawless piece of rock crystal. He lifted it out, turning it tenderly in his hand. It was quite superb! Steeling himself, he replaced it and went downstairs, the box in his hand.

The dealer looked at them, his poker-face betraying no sign of interest. But his eyes betrayed him; he knew the things were magnificent. "These are nice! Pretty little things, aren't they? Chinese, I suppose. Tourist-trade stuff, I expect. Late nineteenth century, wouldn't you say? Nicely carved, though. Not in my line, of course." He was aware that Jabez knew he was lying in virtually every particular, but it amused him to tease the man a little before making his derisory offer. "All right then, Japanese, and good quality. But still not my line. Tell you what, though—there's a feller I know in Bournemouth; he deals in oriental bits and pieces. Gives a fair price, I suppose—thirty or forty quid apiece for decent netsuke. Course, there's lots of fakes about and I don't know enough about them to tell. I wouldn't risk more than a few quid. If he's not interested I'd be stuck with them. Just like you've been!" He gave a light laugh.

Jabez flinched as if struck. These were very fine netsuke and the man knew it. They were worth several times the paltry offer he was finally compelled to accept. He tried to barter, but the hand he had to play was weak. The dealer could bide his time; the old man needed money urgently. These smarmy dealers came and rooked him at will because they could get to him so easily, whereas he was unable to shop around for a decent price amongst reputable businesses in the city. He had often stood at the door of his shop, wistfully watching the constant steam of potential customers as they passed along the by-pass less than quarter of a mile away. Until that new stretch of road had been opened his shop had been popular and profitable, reputable buyers and sellers of antiques calling regularly to see him. Now only the occasional "shark" appeared.

Ninety-five pounds in cash was the final offer, and Jabez had no choice but to accept. The man produced a wallet, which he carefully shielded from Jabez's curious eye. Taking out a slim wad of notes, he slid the wallet back into his pocket and began to count the money onto the drum table in the centre of the room. "Forty-five pounds. Now, just give me half a mo', there's some petrol money I keep in the van." He left the shop and rummaged in the front of his Range Rover.

He returned with profuse but patently insincere apologies. "There," he said placing more notes on top of the existing pile. "Seventy-five. That's all I have on me." *Liar!* thought Jabez Gould. "But I'll tell you what I'll do with you—seventy-five in 'readies' and I'll throw in a very fine antique shop window dummy I just bought over in Chelmsford. Period, it is. I could get a very fair price for it, but I'm just on my way to pick up some nice bits of furniture, and it would be a bit of a squeeze getting them in the back with the dummy in there. Big demand for dummies like that in the up-market rag-trade at present. You'd have no trouble getting fifty or sixty "notes" for it. Seventy-five's all I've got on me, honest. Unless you want a cheque, that is. But that would have to go through the books, like, and I'd have to think about the deal..." He tapped the side of his nose and winked. "Well, that's my offer, then—seventy-five and the dummy. How about it?"

So it was that Jabez and the dealer had lugged the rough crate through the shop and into the kitchen earlier in the day. When the man had gone, Jabez Gould brewed himself a pot of watery tea, still lamenting the loss of his exquisite little Japanese carvings.

The next day he settled one or two of his most pressing debts before opening the shop late in the morning. As he wound up the old-fashioned blind, sunlight frosted the window with a silvery patina. He looked round the dingy shop and was saddened at the sight. Half-heartedly he cleaned the window, inside and out, then busied himself by washing some of his stock of ceramics and glassware. He vacuumed the threadbare carpet, dusted the shelves and applied a beeswax polish to the best of the furniture he had for sale. The drum table was undoubtedly the most valuable amongst them.

His chores were not completed until early evening. The shop door had been propped open all day, but not a soul had entered. He slid aside a heavy lump of Cumbrian haematite which served as his door-stop. Its dark chestnut surface gleamed as rays from the setting sun spangled its lewd organic shape. It rested next to an umbrella stand, looking out of place, like a lump of offal; "Kidney Ore"—it was well named. Specimens of such form and texture were now very scarce, but he knew he would not get more than a few pounds for a large well-shaped example worth over a hundred to a mineral collector. He shook his head softly as he closed and locked the door.

Although now reasonably clean, his shop contained little to admire. In truth, he could no longer regard himself as an antique dealer. He had become reduced to the status of a knowledgeable junk-merchant. Through his hands had passed some magnificent items; splendid furniture, exotic carpets, fine silverware, enamelled glass, mirrors set in gilded frames. At one time he had been an acknowledged authority on English equestrian paintings. Small wonder that it was with increasing reluctance that he now entered his own "showroom", where all that remained was some tawdry furniture and bygones, with a selection of inferior bits of crockery on shelves which had once proudly held Bow, Chelsea early Worcester and Wheildon.

For two days the dummy remained in its plank coffin. He could hardly ignore its existence since it occupied much of the available floor-space in his kitchen. Something would have to be done about it

He was still staring morosely at the crate when the jangle of the doorbell shattered the silence. He started at the sound, put down the tea-towel he was holding, and entered the shop. A pretty girl stood in the doorway, closing her umbrella, apologising for the trickle of water which was draining from her nylon coat onto the worn Axminster carpet. He waved her embarrassment aside. "It doesn't matter, really it doesn't." And really, it didn't.

She started to look round the room. She stooped to examine a stack of old gramophone records. With a cry of delight, she lifted one from the pile, slid it deftly from its cardboard sleeve and examined it, taking care not to touch the playing surface with her slender fingers. Clearly she was used to handling records. "How much is this?" she asked excitedly.

He took it from her, donning his gold-framed spectacles. It was Busoni, playing his beloved Bach. He considered for a moment before replying. "I'm afraid these records were not really intended for sale. You see they are part of my own collection—I bought them in here the other day, intending to have a sort through them—but somehow never got round to it. He glanced at her, and noted the crestfallen expression. "This is something rather special. Busoni made surprisingly few gramophone records. He was one of the major pianists who espoused the cause of the player-piano. When I had the big shop in Malvern I had a 'Duo-Art' reproducer-piano. Great big thing. Electric-powered, of course. Weighed a ton! Used to have scores of rolls for it, including some of Busoni's." He sighed, his unfocused eyes staring into a remote past.

"I have a CD compilation of a lot of his performances. But it's not like having the real thing, is it?" She held up the record shyly.

He stared at the girl, then smiled. "Indeed, it is not," he agreed. "This record has given me a great deal of pleasure. However, it's a pleasure which should now perhaps be enjoyed by someone else. Is there any particular reason you chose this disc?"

"Well, it is on the compilation I have, but somehow it's just so thrilling to hold one of the actual discs he made back in the 1920s. This is something to treasure..."

He nodded. How refreshing! A real enthusiast who genuinely wanted something for its own sake—not merely to exploit for profit. Thoughts of the netsuke still rankled. "Just a moment, I've got lots more in the back place. There's some Hoffman, lots of Cortot, of course, and one real rarity—two one-sided discs of the first movement of Grieg's piano concerto played by Backhaus. It was the first attempt to record a piano concerto, way back in 1909! This recording isn't in any of the lists of his recordings that I've ever seen. Nothing more than a novelty now, of course, but it was a sensation in its day. I couldn't possibly let you have that, though—a modern 78 rpm needle would ruin it in a single playing. Records like this have to be played with a triangular bamboo 'needle' or one made from a thorn. Such needles were produced commercially in the early days of recording. Anyway, you're welcome to have a look through my collection. If anything takes your fancy, we'll think about the price."

The girl hesitated. "I'm afraid I've got very little with me, but I can call again. You see, I only came in on impulse ..."

"And to get out of the rain, no doubt!" he chuckled without rancour.

She looked somewhat abashed, then smiled softly. "Yes, that was the real reason, to be perfectly honest. But I'm glad I did," she said, patting the record softly.

She left twenty minutes later, clutching in one hand several records in a plastic bag, and in the other her umbrella. She turned and smiled cheerfully to the old man through the shop window before hurrying from sight along the wet pavement. For the first time since that dealer had called, Jabez Gould was happy. The girl, a music student who had recently moved into the district, had emptied her purse onto his table; a couple of pounds, some silver and a few pennies. Her face had been a study; she wanted those records, wanted them badly. Would he keep them on one side for her? She would call back, soon...

He had swept up the little heap of coins and dropped them back into her purse, then, raising a finger to his lips, he had put the records into a bag for her. "Let's hear no more about it," he had said. Her face lit up and, impulsively, she kissed the old man's furrowed cheek. Jabez straightened his back and smiled—antique dealer once more. That girl had given him back some self-respect, ample payment for a few old records.

As he stood in the shop, an idea began to form in his mind. Not *everything* he had was junk. He would weed out the dross, hide it in the unused dining room. Only the best would be on show. Pensively he returned to the back room.

A little later he removed the sack-cloth from the shop-window dummy and saw it for the first time. It was wearing corduroy trousers and a coarse Norfolk jacket, ravaged by the moth. The incongruous dancing pumps gleamed from the turned-up cuffs of the corduroys. The face was pockmarked where several patches of brittle paint had flaked from the wooden head. With some difficulty he hauled the dummy from the box, surprised by its weight and rigidity. Stripping off the ruined clothing, he examined the figure closely. It was beautifully made, with intricate metal joints that could be locked in any position by means of brass wing-nuts. The arms, legs and neck could be shortened or extended by adjusting telescopic tubes, which also allowed them to be removed when changing the clothing it was to wear. A small oval of pressed silvery metal was fixed to the centre of the dummy's back, just below the neck, with tiny brass pins. The raised inscription read:

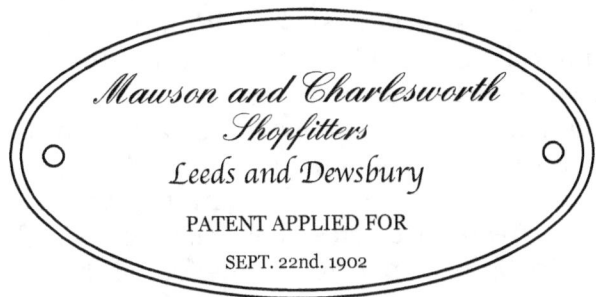

Mawson and Charlesworth
Shopfitters
Leeds and Dewsbury
PATENT APPLIED FOR
SEPT. 22nd. 1902

Junk it might be; unsalable, at least in his shop, it certainly was. And yet, in its own way, it was a very admirable object. Going to his cupboard, he took out some dusters and a small wooden box containing a selection of tiny tins of enamel paint.

By nightfall the dummy was thoroughly cleaned and polished. The joints had been greased with petroleum jelly and the marks on the face skillfully over-painted. the old man stood back, spectacles on forehead, and surveyed his handiwork with satisfaction. The dealer had been right after all—forty pounds was indeed a low price for this well made, rather interesting Edwardian curio. However, the price he had paid was purely academic, since he would never be able to sell it.

The next day he woke early. Beyond his window a flotilla of pure white clouds bobbed at anchor in the clear blue sky, the bright sunlight highlighting their edges with silver wire. He rose and dressed.

Half an hour later he was clambering up a rickety ladder into the attic, where he was greeted with the familiar, reassuring smell of saddle soap and old paper; musty, but not damp. He thrust himself through the narrow trapdoor, then paused, allowing his eyes to become accustomed to the meagre light that filtered through the dull glass of a dormer window. Carefully avoiding several heaps of books, an ancient typewriter and a couple of cabin trunks, he made his way to a large wicker hamper which stood in a dark corner of the room. He dragged it over the dusty floorboards until it lay under the little window. Unfastening the leather straps, he tipped back the lid, which hit the floor with a thump.

Inside, shrouded in tissue paper were neatly folded bundles of antiquated clothing, most of which had belonged to a great-uncle. He opened each package with care, exclaiming with satisfaction from time to time as he searched methodically through the hamper. At length he rose, having made his selection. After repacking the unwanted residue, he hauled the creaking basket back to its accustomed place and ferried his booty down to the kitchen.

The dummy lay stiffly on the floor, its back against the wooden crate. Jabez heaved the figure onto a battered day-bed in the dining room where there was more space in which to work, and laid out its new finery. His great-uncle had established a moderately successful import business, but the opulence of his formal dress reflected his aspirations rather than his actual social standing.

Soon the dummy sported a white silk shirt, over which was fitted a detachable shirt-front, stiff as plaster-of-Paris, and featuring a row of non-functional, globular "pearl" buttons rather reminiscent of silver cake decorations gone dull. With considerable difficulty he fitted a bow tie of black silk, then inched a pair of immaculate trousers over its "long Johns". The waistcoat and swallow-tailed jacket were soon in place and the arms locked in place with their *patent-applied-for* sockets. Socks and shoes were coaxed onto the slender feet and a neatly-folded handkerchief tucked into its breast pocket. Where necessary he padded the figure with crumpled paper. A gold watch-chain with an elaborate fob was looped across the waistcoat to secure a half-hunter watch, which he placed in the little front pocket. On impulse, he removed the watch, wound it and set it to the correct time before slipping it back into the pocket.

His work on the dummy completed for the moment, he moved into the shop. The large, irregularly faded sun-blind which covered the entire window allowed only a little light to penetrate, and instead of raising it, he turned on the light. The "Closed" sign hung lopsidedly at the window in the outer door. He drew a small buff-coloured curtain over the glass and was ready to begin his work.

For the next hour and a half he was very busy shifting most of his stock from the room. Most of the furniture he manhandled into the dining room, along with smaller items packed in boxes, which he stacked by the wall.

Having created a large clear space, he planned his next moves with care. The drum table was covered with a richly-embroidered maroon table-cloth. A Victorian balloon-backed chair was retrieved from the dining room and placed beside it. Then, using the "fireman's lift", he hoisted the dummy from its day bed and carried it into the shop. With a grunt, he lowered it onto the chair then tightened the wing-nuts through the thickness of its clothing. He was dissatisfied with its posture, the arms dangling by its sides. It was rather top-heavy, and appeared liable to topple from the horsehair seat at any moment. With its arms placed on the table and locked in place, it looked much more at ease, but Jabez was still not happy. Eventually he replaced the balloon-back with a padded chair of cane and wicker, which he pulled close to the table once the dummy was installed. Much better, he decided, retightening the wing nuts.

The old man relaxed for a moment. Standing with his back to the window, he surveyed the tableau he had created. The overall effect was ruined by the empty shelves on the walls behind. With a sigh, he took a screwdriver and removed all but the narrow one running eighteen inches below the ceiling, which had been specially installed to display his once fine collection of dinner-plates. He put back the best of his wares, and they looked reasonably presentable.

After a belated lunch, he took a critical look at the scene, and was forced to conclude that the effect was now spoiled by the worn-out Axminster carpet. With a shrug of resignation, he cleared everything to one side, rolled up the carpet and dragged it through the house and into the little yard at the back. Then he clambered back into the attic, and unearthed another of his treasures, a large Persian carpet. Years ago, this had been carefully rolled on a large cardboard tube and wrapped in a dust sheet. He dragged it to the trap-door and cautiously lowered it down the ladder. The smell of mothballs became almost overpowering as he unrolled it in the shop. When it was installed, and the furniture replaced, the effect proved to have been worth the effort. The dummy was beginning to look at home, he felt.

He was a little disappointed on entering the shop the following morning. The faded, nondescript wallpaper was badly marred by marks left by the shelving. It really should be re-papered, but he was sure that he would not be able to obtain any modern paper which would be appropriate. There was a possible alternative, however...

The attic yielded several lengths of dark green baize. He cut them to length, nailed them to the plate shelves, and draped them to form loose swags over the wall. It was a strenuous task, and he was not entirely convinced by the final appearance. Still, it was an improvement. The room looked cosier for his efforts.

The electric light struck a discordant note, and he soon returned from the dining room with an impressive oil-lamp, which he kept filled with paraffin in case of power cuts. He struck a match and lit the broad wick, then adjusted the flame until the black smoke disappeared. Shadows lurched around him as he moved towards the table and placed the lamp before the dummy. The warm, living flame produced an almost magical transformation in the little room.

And so the old man's self-imposed labours continued. By the end of the day he had gathered together a remarkable quantity of outmoded furnishings and bric-a-brac, which he arranged with care to recreate the atmosphere of an Edwardian bachelor's apartment. He slumped into the balloon chair, which he had drawn up to the table and glanced at the face of the dummy. In the gentle light of the oil lamp its supercilious expression seemed to have mellowed a little and its painted eyes to sparkle with a hint of suppressed amusement. The old man produced a crumpled packet of cigarettes and lit one.

Relaxing in his chair, he became aware of the disturbing sensation of being watched. Glancing up, he saw with a shock that the head of the dummy was turning slowly away from him. He half rose from his chair, his heart fluttering with the unexpected movement. Calming himself, he moved to the dummy's side, removed the starched shirt-front, opened the buttons beneath and reached into the cavity. His probing fingers located the locking-nut at the neck. It had worked loose, the ancient screw-thread being very worn. He adjusted the head then re-tightened the wing-nut, applying as much pressure as he was able in the confined space. The strain proved too great for the brass thread, which stripped, allowing the head to swivel to one side again. He cursed with annoyance, then tearing the thick backing from an old calendar he made a wedge, which he jammed firmly between the base of the head and the shoulder piece. It stayed in position, so he re-fastened the shirt and fixed the front in place.

His cigarette had burned away to an insubstantial caterpillar of ash on the glass tray. He lit another before extinguishing the lamp and making his way from the room.

The next day was cold and windy, with fine drizzle pattering spasmodically against the window. Jabez rose reluctantly, and having risen, dressed hurriedly, standing on the bare linoleum by the side of his bed.

He made himself a pot of tea in the kitchen, but as the table was piled with stacks of books, bits of crockery and other odds and ends he took his drink into the shop. It was very dark, the heavy green drapes absorbing what little light percolated through the midnight-blue blind at the window. After lighting the lamp, he picked up the soggy newspaper, which had just flopped onto the mat by the door and placed it on the table beside his tray. Glancing at the dummy, he noted with satisfaction that his makeshift wedge had held.

"Good morning," he remarked aloud. "Although whether it's good or bad doesn't matter a damn to you, does it?" The dummy ignored him, its haughty face registering faint disdain. Jabez slurped his tea. He stabbed a finger at the paper, observing acidly "Councillor Thomlins has come up with another of his schemes. The Council slapped a compulsory purchase order on the old brewery and demolished it a couple of years back. Supposed to be for housing. Now he wants to let a developer build an amusement arcade there. He's as bent as Harry Lauder's walking-stick, you mark my words." He glanced at his silent companion, to find himself confronted by those piercing dark eyes again. The cardboard wedge must have slipped a bit.

He examined the dummy's eyes; they were remarkably life-like, he thought as he stared into the jet-black pupils. They seemed to expand as he leaned forward. Larger and larger they grew until they appeared like twin pools of pitch. He seemed drawn to the left eye, which yawned before him, expanding until he felt that he must fall, spinning and whirling, into its unplumbed depths. His knuckles went white and he grasped the edge of the table to prevent himself from falling. Then, in an instant, the awful spasm of vertigo passed. Clutching a hand to his forehead, he stumbled from the table and returned to the kitchen. He sat down heavily on the only vacant chair, shaken and quivering.

After lunch he re-entered the shop, where he was startled to discover that the dummy had slumped a little in the wicker chair and appeared to be staring intently at the newspaper with those clear, unflinching eyes. Jabez shivered. It was cold in the room. The cast iron fireplace, with its marble surround, had been completely obscured for many years by the tall bookcase which now stood in the dining room. It was a very attractive Queen Anne style fireplace, which, if cleaned and polished, should become the focal point of the room once more. And he would light if for the first time in perhaps a dozen years.

He rummaged through the cupboard under the kitchen sink, and eventually discovered an unopened tin of Zeebo oven polish. He shook it and was delighted to hear the thick liquid slopping about inside. He shook it vigorously, and with the aid of a pair of pliers, unscrewed its knurled lid.

It proved to be perfectly usable, and after he had cleaned the slight traces of rust from the grate he began to apply the pungent liquid. It was a good, clean smell, and he started to whistle cheerfully as the metal took on a rich silver-black lustre. As he paused to unscrew the lid again, he heard a distinct creak behind him. Had someone quietly entered the shop, or come through from the kitchen? No, that was impossible, the doors were locked, and the shop-door bell on its long swan-necked spring had remained silent. Snatching up the poker, he swivelled round and rose to his feet. No one was there.

He stood by the hearth, confused and embarrassed by his own nervousness. Only then did he realise that the dummy had slumped still further into its chair, and was regarding him with an expression of cruel amusement. He threw down the poker and moved to the table. Those confounded joints needed tightening properly. He reached towards the dummy before realising, just in time, that his hands were covered with grate polish. Cursing under his breath, he looked from his hands to the dummy's immaculate attire. "Damn!" he said, and resumed his task at the fire. But, as he worked, he was strangely aware of those intense eyes which were trained on his back as he crouched by the hearth.

The room looked much more homely when the fire was lit in the prim little semi-circular basket. He had scrubbed the Zeebo off his hands and discarded his soiled overall. The dummy sprawled indolently in its chair, appearing to study the open newspaper on the table before it. Jabez was struck by a happy thought, and left the room. Soon he returned, flourishing a vintage newspaper, which he dropped on the table. "There you are," he said with satisfaction. "That's more in line with your interests than the dubious activities of our beloved council. Yes, that's the sort of thing you would have had on your breakfast table." He was thoughtful for a moment. "No, dressed like that you were obviously not at breakfast. All right, then—supper time. That's why the lamp is lit and the curtains drawn."

He readjusted the dummy, placing its elbows on the table and raising its forearms before tightening the various locking-nuts. The slightly clawed hands were raised as if offering a benediction. With a chuckle, the old man opened the stiff, slightly yellowed paper and lodged it between the painted wooden fingers. The newspaper sagged along its centre fold, so he placed the tea-pot behind it to give support. It looked remarkable convincing, the dummy apparently engrossed in the contents of the newspaper.

Jabez regarded the manikin intently. "You know, you look a bit of a 'masher' in that get-up, my lad! A real man-about-town. A bit of a cad, perhaps. I wonder what your name is? Let me see, now… something a bit distinguished. William, perhaps. Or Charles. No, those are ageless, Royal names. It should be something more 'period'. Marmaduke? Better, but still not right…"

Then it came to him in a flash—Archie! Somehow, it could be nothing else. Archie was no aristocrat; rather was he a supercilious, reasonably wealthy young bachelor. He would have sported a silver-headed cane. And gloves. Yes, gloves, most certainly. Archie seemed to nod in agreement as the old man rested his hand lightly on the back of the wicker chair. Soon an ebony stick and a pair of pale lilac gloves lay on the table.

Perhaps Archie would care for some music as he read his paper before going out? The dummy nodded its assent.

Jabez grunted with the weight of the gramophone as he shuffled backwards from the kitchen and lowered it onto a low brass-topped circular table placed close to Archie's side. He returned with the great flaring wooden horn, which he suspended from the spring on its gantry support. He connected the tone-arm, then used a small gadget to cut a new point on a triangular-sectioned slip of bamboo. He inserted the needle into the clamp of the sound-box, then wound the handle, taking care to release the brake mechanism first to minimise the risk of snapping the spring. When it was fully wound, he reapplied the brake, selected one of his favourite records and placed it on the turn-table. He adjusted the turn-table speed indicator to eighty rpm, ran a padded plush cleaner gently round the grooves and was ready to play the record. He released the brake and with infinite care, lowered the needle into the groove.

There was a short faint hiss, then the glorious voice of Madam Tetrazzini rang out with bell-like clarity in the Jewel Song from Faust. Jabez listened, enthralled, closing his eyes as he sat in the balloon-backed chair. The pathetically thin quality of the orchestral accompaniment served only to emphasise the thrilling voice that cascaded from the disc.

There was a loud crash, the voice vanished and Jabez was jolted back to reality. He leaped to his feet and stared in horror at the shattered record. Archie had slipped sideways, his right hand dropping from the table and smashing down onto the unprotected disc.

There was anger as well as sorrow in the old man's heart as he collected up the shards of the precious record and placed them in the kitchen bin. He went back into the room, hauled Archie's stiff body back into position. He wedged it more firmly in place with a couple of cushions before tightening the nuts once more, this time using pliers. The dummy's haughty expression seemed to betray the faintest suggestion of a sneer.

Jabez glowered back. "Madam Tetrazzini not to your taste, then? All right, just let me see." He sorted through the pile of records and produced an Edwardian parlour ballad sung by Mr. Ernest Pike. He repeated his preparations at the gramophone, then the small room resounded to the fervent declamations of the tenor. Jabez did not close his eyes this time. He watched, fascinated as Archie's head turned almost imperceptibly towards the gramophone. Its changed position relative to the lamp had banished the earlier sneer, and the wooden face seemed to register guarded approval; Archie liked the record—"The Roses of Picardy".

It was then that Jabez Gould began to feel like an interloper in the shop he had occupied for so many years. He looked round the room, feeling more an unwelcome visitor than the proprietor. The neglected, untidy shop had gradually been transformed into a very convincing reconstruction of an Edwardian parlour. Practically everything within the room was authentic and of the right period and had been arranged with the insight which comes from long experience of handling antiques. The very photographs on the mantelpiece, the record spinning on the ancient gramophone, the scrapbook lying on the beadwork foot-rest, the coal-fire burning in the grate behind the polished brass fender—every detail had been chosen with great care. Even the books in the what-not had been specially selected to the taste of the slightly arrogant figure seated at the table. The shop had evolved into Archie's room, and the wooden dummy seemed far more at ease and in keeping with the decor than the old man himself.

A slight tremor passed through the body of Jabez Gould. With downcast eyes he retreated slowly from the room and did not enter it again that day. He went about his business like an automaton, making the remainder of his domain more habitable. He tumbled into bed that night worried and exhausted.

· · · · · ·

He woke in the small hours with a sense of foreboding. Something was wrong...

Switching on the light, he rose and donned his camel-hair dressing gown. There was a faint, indefinable sound from the rooms below. There was a slight creak followed by a rustling sound; then silence. Opening his wardrobe, he took out a heavy stick. Turning out the light, he cautiously swung back the door and began to creep down the dark stair. With pounding heart he reached the seventh step—halfway. There was a loud rasping sound, then the voice of Ernest Pike rang out in the deathly silence. The old man, startled, hesitated, his stick raised defiantly above his head. He resisted the temptation to retreat and barricade himself into his room and resumed his stealthy descent.

He paused at the door of Archie's room, and could see a crack of light emerging from the gap at its foot. Grasping the door handle firmly in his left hand, he turned it slowly and smoothly until he knew that the catch was free. Suddenly he flung the door open and rushed in, his stick poised to strike.

Once inside he stopped abruptly, his heart pounding. The oil-lamp was burning, and the fire blazed brightly in the hearth—but the room was unoccupied save for Archie, whose head was turned towards the intruder. Ernest Pike's song came to an end, and the needle swung into the "dead track" where it rasped and clicked a meaningless regular beat.

Jabez moved across the room and applied the rim brake. He was utterly perplexed and deeply disturbed. He had no recollection of having made up the fire, which appeared to have been recently stoked, and felt certain that he could not have left the lamp burning. But it was the business of the gramophone which bothered him most. Desperately he tried to rationalise the problem. It was conceivable that he could absent-mindedly have rewound the machine, and placed the needle into the groove, inexplicably failing to release the brake. Some vibration, a change in the temperature of the room, perhaps, could have caused the brake to slip. He tested it. It appeared to be in perfect order.

Had he, then, taken to sleepwalking? He could, quite unwittingly, have lit the lamp, made up the fire and started the gramophone himself. That must be the solution. Then he realised that the theory would not wash; the record had commenced whilst he was half-way down the stairs—yet these old machines had no sort of repeating mechanism. One possible explanation remained—someone was playing a practical joke. He went round the entire house, checking every window catch and the locks and bolts on the doors. Everything was as it should be...

He returned to Archie's room. For a moment he stood watching the inert form, then sat down on his chair, facing it. He gazed at its painted eyes, fixing them with his own. The dummy stared insolently back at him. With rising fury he raised his stick, knocked aside the newspaper and prodded Archie firmly in the chest. The gleaming shirt-front flexed. He jabbed again. This time the front slid aside, and the tip of his stick ripped a hole through the ripe silk of the shirt, penetrating into the chest cavity in the region of the heart. As the point tore through the thin fabric, the dummy fell back, its mocking expression instantly replaced by one of hatred.

Aghast, the old man rose from the table, knocking over his own chair, which fell with a crash against the fender. Surely the change in the dummy's expression was more than a mere trick of the light? He retreated, holding the stick, quivering, in front of him like a sword. Edging backwards, he made his way from the room and closed the door thankfully behind him. There was a heavy bolt at the top of the door. It had not been used in years, and was thick with rust. Frantically he hammered the projecting ball of the bar upwards with the heel of his hand, oblivious to the pain and the blood which spurted from a ragged gash in his palm. At last the bolt entered its socket. He was safe.

Ashen-faced, he stumbled into the kitchen. The wound was already throbbing. He wrapped a clean tea-towel around it as tightly as he was able. Then he climbed up to one of the high cupboards and produced a small bottle of brandy. He opened it with difficulty, and poured a generous measure into a tea-cup. He gulped it down, almost gagging as the fiery liquid burned its way down his throat. He poured another...

Some time later he sprawled on the day-bed, a hearth-rug pulled over him.

• • • • • •

It was broad daylight when he awoke. His hand ached abominably, and he had a hangover. He forced his eyes to focus, then rose from his makeshift bed. The terrifying events of the previous night gradually seeped back into his turbid mind and he reached for the bottle, which lay on its side on the carpet. He stared at it in muddled disbelief. The bottle had not been full, by any means, but surely he could not have drunk all that remained? He ran his left hand over the carpet. There was no trace of moisture; he must have drunk it! Unless...—But no, the thought was madness!

He tottered from the room and examined the bolt on the door to Archie's room. It was firmly in its socket, and on the door jamb and the hall carpet there were trails of dried blood. Suddenly he dashed into the kitchen where he retched violently into the sink.

Afterwards he sat down at the table, cradling his head in his hands. He must have got himself well and truly plastered the night before, all because of that blasted dummy. Then he was struck by a sudden revelation: that horrible experience with Archie and the gramophone did have a rational explanation, after all. The whole episode had been an hallucination caused by the brandy. Similar things had occurred in the past, before he had finally given up the booze.

He made himself some strong black coffee and in a little while his spirits began to revive. With some trepidation he removed the makeshift bandage. He had to soak the last layer free from the great clot of congealed blood on his palm. He was horrified when the pouting purple gash was revealed, along with a series of lesser cuts and bruises. He went to the bathroom cabinet and managed to apply a dressing and a bandage. Really he should see a doctor, or call to the Casualty Department at the hospital, but he felt sure that it would heal itself, given time.

After a bath, a change of clothing and a light lunch he began to feel very much better and realised that he had been acting like a maniac these last few days. What had started out as a bit of imaginative bit of window-dressing had developed into an obsession. Somehow that confounded dummy had taken over; had ousted him from his own shop, had induced him to slam the bolt with his bare hand. More to the point, it had driven him to a state of drunken stupor for the first time in many years. Archie, the outmoded brainchild of Messrs Mawson and Charlesworth, would have to go. At once!

As he stood at the door, a hammer gripped carefully in his injured hand, ready to release the bolt, he was struck by a sudden sense of foreboding. He was tempted to creep away, but that would serve only to postpone the confrontation. Steeling himself, he tapped the head of the bolt several times. Gradually it slid back from the socket. The door was free. He squared his shoulders and turned the handle.

The lamp and the fire were both out. He turned on the light. Archie sprawled at the table, one gloved hand resting on the base of the ornate lamp. The overturned balloon-back chair lay with its top resting on the pierced brass fender. He righted it and placed it by the table.

Taking Archie firmly by the shoulders, he dragged the dummy back against the wickerwork, noting the displaced shirt front and the ragged tear beneath. God, he really must have been drunk! Carefully removing the dummy's clothing piece by piece, he folded the costume neatly in a pile on the Persian rug beside him. Once the dummy was completely stripped, and its appendages locked back in place, he grasped it by the ankles and dragged it from the room, through the hall and kitchen, down the steps and into the yard, where he had already deposited the crate and the old shop carpet.

It was with a strange sense of satisfaction that he took the trouble to replace Archie's incongruous garb before hauling the dummy back into its crate. Covering it once more with the dirty bit of sacking, he returned to the kitchen and closed the door behind him. Blood was oozing from the now soiled dressing on his hand, which was throbbing with pain. Yet he felt a great sense of relief. He was almost cheerful again; Archie had gone! He would quietly rot away, un-mourned, in the yard. Even better, Jabez decided, he would make a bonfire with the crate and totally destroy the hateful object which had brought him nothing but misfortune.

After re-dressing his hand, he made himself a couple of sandwiches. He ate them at the drum table, sitting in Archie's chair. No - his own chair, dammit! and listened to a selection of his favourite records. It really was very pleasant sitting there alone in the opulent room listening to the gramophone. He should have closed up the shop years ago and done just this. He lit the table lamp and turned out the harsh electric light. It was beginning to get a little chilly. He raked out the grate, re-laid the fire and lit it. Soon there was a cheerful blaze and he added more coal from the helmet-shaped brass scuttle. After some hesitation he went down into the cellar and returned with a small bottle of wine. Might as well do it in style, just this once. To celebrate, he told himself. He returned to the kitchen for a corkscrew. There he noticed his great-uncle's clothing, which he had stripped from the body of the usurper. A gleam came to his eye...

The jacket was a trifle short in the sleeve, but otherwise the outfit might have been made for him. Once the stiff shirt front was in place, there was no sign of the tear over his heart. He returned to the table, placing down the corkscrew and a very elegant 18th Century baluster glass with a sparkling air-twist in its stem. He poured a drop of the wine and sampled it. "You may pour," he declared.

Resplendent in his great-uncle's finery, he raised his glass. "To Archie! I will eat, drink and be merry; for tomorrow, he dies," he said with a chuckle.

Dame Nellie Melba serenaded him as he picked up the newspaper he had selected for the benefit of the ousted dummy. "Manchester Guardian, June 15th., 1905" he commented, picking it up. The front page was entirely taken up with small advertisements, as was customary at that time. "Ah well, no news was always good news," he quipped, turning the page.

The smile drained from his lips as his eyes lighted on another, larger advertisement, with an engraved illustration of a shop dummy. "Messrs Mawson and Charlesworth, Shopfitters and Undertakers, established 1872," he read. Below the banner was the picture of Archie, wearing a formal dress-suit. His curled mustachios and the piercing eyes were unmistakable. He flung the paper to the floor and poured another glass of wine. Archie was not going to ruin another night for him.

Somewhat later he produced a small packet of cigars from a drawer in the dining room. He extracted one, held it to his ear and rolled it backwards and forwards between his fingers. It was a little dry, but welcome nevertheless. He rose unsteadily from his chair and leaned to light it at the tip of the tall glass chimney of the lamp. As he did so the silence was broken by a sudden hiss from the gramophone, then the sonorous voice of Ernest Pike flooded the room. Jabez swiveled, confused and frightened. He certainly hadn't put that damned record on again. He couldn't have done...

As he turned he caught a glimpse of himself in the over mantle mirror, and stifled the scream which welled up inside him: the face was not his own! It was pallid and was embellished with neatly-curled mustachios. The piercing eyes that glared back at him were the painted eyes of the shop dummy.

He lunged at the gramophone, bumping heavily against the top of the drum table. The oil lamp tilted, then with agonising slowness, it toppled, smashing onto the rug. Gouts of flaming paraffin gushed over the floor, leaped to the heavy drapes and transformed them instantly to inverted torrents of flame. He staggered back, losing his balance as he knocked against the low gramophone table. As he fell, his head crashed against the fender and he knew no more.

· · · · · ·

Miraculously, the fire was short-lived. A young music student returning from a concert was passing the shop on her bicycle as the window-blind burst into flames. She called the fire brigade from a nearby telephone box, and few minutes later a fire tender blared its way from the by-pass and wove its way down the twisting old road. The men quickly brought the fire under control, managing to confine it to the shop area. Sadly, the only occupant, an elderly man, was declared dead on arrival at the hospital.

Sent to examine the rear of the premises, one of the firemen broke down the tall wooden gate into the yard, and almost fell over a large narrow crate. Dragging aside the sacking, he shone his torch into it, and for one horrifying moment, thought that he had discovered a second corpse. Then he realised with relief that the handsome face was merely that of an old shop-window dummy, whose eyes appeared to blink as the light swept over its painted eyes. "I wonder what will happen to you? Down the tip, I expect," the man muttered, dropping the cover back over the face and continued with his investigation.

Under the sacking, Archie glowered in silence.

Persistence of the Anima

The fate of the old *Beaumaris Castle* survey ship was sealed a few hours before the start of her 23rd mission, when a hairline fracture in the field-coil stabiliser remained undetected during the routine pre-flight inspection.

Forty-seven days into the voyage a tell-tale light began to flash and the klaxon to wail. Moments later, a violent implosion shattered the heart of the ship. A wave of nausea, the inevitable side effect of the rapid starting or stopping of a quantum-drive motor, prostrated her crew of four men and a woman for some minutes. Still retching, Jamieson, the ship's engineer, scrambled through the elliptical entrance to the command capsule where a woozy Commander Read was studying the engine-pit monitors. The blurred images confirmed their worst fears. Through the rippling haze of the ebbing field, he could discern an amorphous mass of wreckage suspended in the centre of the pit.

Like most progressive captains, Read believed in "Command by Consensus." Although at the end of the day the buck stopped with him, he gave full consideration to the views and opinions of his colleagues. The conference was brief—few options were available for discussion....

Nine days later the *Castle* went into orbit some two hundred and thirty miles above the surface of a small jade jewel of a planet. Survey instrumentation chattered busily in the observation turret. Close-ups of the surface appeared on the video plate. Read and his crew peered intently at the images. Much of the land surface was lush with vegetation and there was a great blue ocean, reminiscent of old Earth.

Beaumaris Castle began her approach. The skin temperature rose rapidly, increasing the strain on plating already stressed by the implosion. A barely discernible crack appeared in the outer skin. It extended in short bursts, then doubled back on itself. As the ship flipped gracefully upwards ready for the final descent, there was a loud crack and a ragged shard of plasteel burst from the shell. The *Beaumaris Castle* began to spin slowly as she descended.... Miraculously, the landing was violent but not catastrophic. Somehow, she remained upright. Captain and crew, naturally, had donned their armoured supraphane spacesuits before the descent. Read led them out from the airlock, and found himself standing in a saucer-shaped depression several hundred yards in diameter. In the distance a range of pale blue hills was outlined against a golden sky of shot-silk. The branches of trees and shrubs rose over the lip of the plain.

Margaret Thurnam dropped to the ground, her squeal of delight echoing through the helmets of her companions as she plucked something from the ground and held it up to her visor. What had appeared to be turf proved to be a dense covering of a moss-like plant. Read produced a small instrument from his thigh-pouch and clicked it on. It indicated that the atmosphere was perfectly breathable. Cautiously he unclipped his visor, ready to slam it back in an instant. He took a shallow breath. Sharp fresh air entered his space-stale lungs. Grinning, he held up both thumbs. Reassured, the others followed his example. Jamieson leaped high into the air brandishing a fist in triumph. "Lords of all we survey," he yelled, then sank to his knees on the deep springy moss. Read laughed inanely as the pressure of his lonely command fell from his shoulders. Then he sank to his knees, tears of relief welling in his eyes. Against all odds, he had brought them to safety; now it was up to Margaret Thurnam....

At length the party rose from the slightly iridescent carpet of moss. A pale cyclamen-coloured sun hung high over the distant mountains. No animals gambolled on the plain, but a lone opalescent creature resembling a two-winged butterfly flapped past several feet above their heads. The biologist chased futilely after it, her long hair streaming back over her clumsy suit. She did not seem to appreciate that since descending the short ladder from the ship, she had assumed command of the mission. Read walked to her side and quietly reminded her of the pertinent clause in Company Regulations. For a moment she looked startled, then flashed a dazzling smile. "Whatever you say, Skip!" He laughed with her.

They took stock of their situation. They had sustained no injuries from the hard landing, and were all in high spirits. There were still sufficient rations for a few weeks, and they were eager to explore. Jamieson returned to the ship for the rations. Then from his tool locker he retrieved the bottle of wine he had smuggled aboard and slipped it into his backpack along with five Sterilene mugs, wishing he had thought to smuggle aboard some decent wineglasses as well. They had ample cause to celebrate.

He slung the biologist's Pocket-Lab over his shoulder, and added a razor-sharp cook's knife and five laser-pen guns to the selection of other weapons in his pack. Although the Pocket-Lab did not quite justify its name, it was a very compact unit, and it would prove invaluable for testing such potential foodstuffs as they might find. Thurnam took it from him and hung it casually from her shoulder. "By the way," he informed her, "I hooked up the ship's homing beacon to the main power supply. Even if the recovery ship takes longer than we expect, it will still be able to pinpoint us." An automatic "Mayday" call had been initiated when the implosion occurred.

"I should have thought of that," she replied morosely. The homing beacon's own power supply had a limited life, but connected to the mains, it would continue to broadcast for at least a year. Their suit-receivers were tuned to the same frequency, allowing them to wander at will, yet always able find their way back, even in total darkness.

Jamieson handed out the packs of food and canteens of water before laying a selection of weapons on the moss. Each took a laser pen pistol. Read also picked up a web-gun and a folding knife. All had collecting bags. "Now let's see what we can find for the stock-pot," Thurnam said, leading the party towards the rim of the landing site. She looked back just once. The old ship, a pockmarked silver statue, stood proud on the benign, alien plain. The ragged hole near the communications shack was just visible; she was astonished that the *Castle* had survived touchdown.

A slight breeze was driving pink-tinged clouds across a cobalt sky paling to gold at the horizon. As five pairs of heavy space-boots crushed the minute feathery fronds, the moss emitted an evocative perfume. Eau de Cologne? Oil of Rosemary, perhaps? The biologist knelt to examine the little plants again, then placed a fragment into the tube of the snifter. "Well," she said, it smells good enough to eat, and it certainly isn't poisonous. I'm going to try it." She discarded her gloves and nipped off a tiny sample. She held it to her tongue, then cautiously nibbled it. An expression of sheer delight spread over her face. "It's like... well, I'm not really sure. It reminds me of something I tasted years ago when I was a kid. Sort of sharp, yet sweet. I know! It's just like apple."

"You tasted apple—real apple—when you were a kid?" jibed Harding.

"Sure, my folks were pretty influential. My mother was an

Ambassador, you know."

"This I have to try!" said Harding, dropping to his feet.

"Me too," cried Jamieson.

"Well, if that's what apple tastes like," declared Read munching happily on the moss, "I see why the red-sash classes keep it to themselves! Of course, we don't know whether it has any real food value, but I could see people back at Rift Colony paying plenty for this! The flavor could be synthesised, I suppose, but not the texture."

"Why don't we fill some of the cargo-crates from the hold with this stuff, and take a trial batch back with us when the Recovery ship arrives?" Costello suggested.

"Well, for one thing, we have no idea how long it will last in store," Thurnam said. "And for another, we've not started exploring yet. As Skip says, it might have no real food-value at all. There might be even better things to discover. Let's get going while we've still got sunlight."

A few minutes later they crested the slight rim of the depression and began to descend a slope. With a cry of delight, Margaret Thurnam leaped forward and stooped to examine a carmine and silver flower shaped like a fluted chalice. It rose almost knee-high, from a tuberous, branching rootstock, like that of an Iris. The men joined her, fascinated by its beauty and its rich perfume. Harding extended his hand, then withdrew it; such beauty should not be wantonly violated. Even the biologist restrained herself, despite her curiosity. Further specimens were soon discovered. Their colours varied enormously, but their six-petalled form was constant. The five space-hardened explorers trod cautiously, ensuring that their boots did not damage any of the nodding flowers, which swayed gently on their long stems. One of the men suggested that they should be marketable as houseplants, and the biologist did not disagree.

As the party resumed its trek down the hill, Read glanced at his ship-time watch, and discovered that it had stopped. He shaded his eyes and looked towards the pastel-hued sun. "Funny," he remarked, the sun doesn't seem to have moved since we arrived. I had the impression it was late afternoon when we started, but it hasn't got any lower. Damn funny. By the way, my watch has stopped. How long have we been going, anybody?"

The others were completely mystified to find that their watches had also stopped. Even stranger, they all registered precisely the same time; they had ceased to function simultaneously. Space-watches had been tried and tested in every possible way. Thurnam shrugged, removed her watch and flung it away. The others laughed, but could not bring themselves to follow her example.

The valley fell away more steeply, and was dotted with small bushes that emerged from the ubiquitous sward of apple-moss. The biologist went to investigate. Meanwhile a light-hearted race started spontaneously amongst the men. Shrieking like schoolboys, the astronauts thundered down the hill, each trying to be the first to reach a small tree they had spotted lower down the slope. Costello's long legs won the day. He flung himself down in a rugby-style tackle at the base of the chosen tree. Read's solid frame hurtled into the prostrate form and they both rolled some way down the slope, laughing inanely.

Costello picked himself up, still giggling as he rose. His laughter ceased abruptly as he realised that he felt no pain from the impact of the Skipper's heavy body. Read's smile also vanished as he too realised that one or both of them should be writhing in agony from their bone-jarring collision. Space-suits, admittedly, were designed for maximum protection, but they could not have cushioned the impact so completely. As Harding reached them, he asked offhandedly "What reading did you get for the gravitational field here?"

"I made it almost three-point-six-five Brailsford—not far off the old Earth Standard. Why?"

"Well, it's just that... Never mind. I just wondered. Anyway, we'd better wait 'til Margaret catches up with us."

She came towards them, holding what appeared to be a handful of varicoloured ostrich plumes. Those ungainly birds had been extinct for ages, even back on Earth, but everyone was familiar with museum specimens or holograms of the things. She handed specimens of the plumes to each of them. "Some sort of fern," she said, sticking hers under the raised visor of her helmet, imparting something of the appearance of a Roman Centurion.

Harding nodded in approval. "I reckon there's a ready-made market for those things, you know. They would be worth a good few Credits in the high-class accessories market at Tielios or Skodon. They are always on the lookout for novelties. We could take a load back with us, so long as they don't fall to bits when they dry out. If they lose their colour they could always be dyed. Anyway, a few crates of these would keep us in drinks for months. He stowed the frond into his collecting bag.

"Talking of drinks," Jamieson remarked, "do you realise that we've been walking for quite some time and we've had nothing to eat or drink since we landed? Well, if anyone's interested, I've got something a little special here…" With the air of a conjurer he slipped the bottle of wine from his pouch and held it up. Strangely enough, the faces of his companions registered only surprise. No one seemed interested.

"Save it until we are ready to do it justice," Margaret Thurnam advised. Jamieson slipped it back into the pouch, rather perplexed.

The biologist removed her helmet, allowing her long chestnut hair to spill over the shoulders of the black suit. She placed the helmet into her collecting-bag, the tip of the feather-fern projecting ludicrously from the top. They resumed their exploration, thankful for the thick treads on their boots, which gave good purchase on the springy moss.

It was Costello who first heard the sound. He stopped instantly, raising a cupped hand to his ear. "Listen…" he said. There was a faint but distinct hissing noise ahead. "I think it is running water, a stream, or a waterfall."

"Certainly sounds like it," the biologist agreed. They walked on in silence, treading as lightly as they could. The sound grew louder as they approached, but they were astonished suddenly to hear a clear cascade of musical notes, a carillon of tiny bells which came from a thicket of tall bushes. It was answered by another peal, then several others joined in until the air was ringing with gossamer-fine curlicues of sound that interlaced in a scintillating counterpoint. The notes rose and fell, trembling, trilling, ebbing and flowing, forming a filigree of unbelievable complexity. The sounds seemed to glitter like a small snowstorm of coloured sequins caught in sunlight. The party froze, mouths agape. Gradually the ethereal sounds died away, and there was a profound silence. The explorers had lapsed into a reverie, each alone in his secret emotion, yet united in a shared experience. Eventually they stirred themselves and resumed their quest.

On reaching the top of a steep wooded ravine they began to edge cautiously down, only to find a sheer ten-metre drop barring their progress. Jamieson, holding onto a convenient branch, leaned out to look down. Suddenly he lost his footing, the branch snapped and he plunged over the edge. Landing at the foot of the ten-metre high rock-face, he was again thankful for the spacesuit, which completely absorbed the impact. He was in a large natural amphitheatre formed by the boles of dozens of splendid trees. Read, who had watched the man's fall with horror, considered for a moment then motioned him away from the base of the cliff, before leaping confidently down. The others quickly followed. Reunited, they made for the group of trees.

Harding glanced back at the cliff, and shook his head; at earth-normal gravity, such a thing was simply not possible....

On reaching the first of the trees, Margaret Thurnam removed a glove and stroked the glass-like bark. She tried scratching it with her nail, then with the point of a folding knife, but was unable to make a mark. Intrigued, she placed the blade firmly against the trunk and drew it across. The bark was still unscathed, but the knife had lost its fine-honed edge. The pocket laser made no impression.

Jamieson produced his heavy cook's knife, placed its point against the bole and struck the handle with a fist-sized chunk of rock. A shard of metal flew off, and he found himself looking ruefully at the shattered tip of the high-tensile steel blade. He looked at Thurnam. "If you are after samples, don't ask for volunteers," he said.

"Well, I'd like a couple of leaves at any rate. And it looks as if there are some fruits up there," she replied, pointing high into the branches.

After several abortive attempts to climb the incredibly slippery trunks of the trees, Costello discovered that the lowest branch of one of the trees was within his reach. He took a leap and managed to haul himself up. He was soon high into its canopy, sitting precariously astride one of its broad limbs, examining a cluster of boat-shaped leaves. He managed to hack one off and dropped it down to the biologist. A little higher up he spotted a cluster of the fruits, and resumed his climb. The perfectly spherical peach-like fruits seemed to glow like red-hot cannon balls. Each was attached to its twig by a web of pale filaments. He removed one carefully, surprised by its lightness, and dropped it to his companions below. He detached several more, then climbed down, confidently dropping the last three or four metres to the ground.

The others were already examining his find. The fruits were enveloped in a brilliantly coloured coating of silky fluff that could be stripped off in sections to reveal a delicious-looking flamingo pink skin beneath. Without bothering to subject it to the snifter, Jamieson, his mouth watering at the prospect, took a generous bite. His expression of drooling anticipation was instantly transformed into one of bewilderment. The "fruit" consisted merely of a thin, fleshy shell which seemed to be nothing more than tasteless wax! He spat it out, whilst the others roared with laughter at his woebegone expression. Once the surprise had worn off, he joined in the laughter, remarking that he wasn't hungry anyway.

Read looked very thoughtful. They must have been away from the ship for several hours, yet no one had touched Jamieson's provisions.

He glanced at his useless watch, then up to the sun, which still hung above the horizon, its pleasant warmth unchanged. They had travelled many miles over difficult terrain, yet they felt no need of rest. His thoughts were interrupted by another peel of the tinkling bells. Again the subtle interplay of sounds trembled through the air. As it faded away, they caught a brief glimpse of a small flock of bird-like creatures before they vanished into the foliage around them.

It was Harding who first noticed the damage to their spacesuits. Small flakes of the black surface were peeling away, and when he examined his helmet in the collecting bag, he discovered that a reticulate pattern of fine grooves had appeared on its surface. Slowly their protective clothing was disintegrating. He detached the visor, staring uncomprehendingly at its deeply pitted surface. He called attention to it, then tossed it to one side. Before long all of their helmets lay on the apple-moss sward. As they walked, a trail of flakes of Supraphane marked their progress.

The sound of running water grew louder as they approached the floor of the main valley. A small cascade of water emerged from a cleft in the rocks to their right. It plunged into a sparkling pool, around which grew lush vegetation. Without a word, and with no sign of embarrassment, Margaret Thurnam stripped off the tattered remains of her space suit, draping it in an untidy heap on a large slab of rock that projected into the water. The men watched, admiring her clean limbs without lust, as she poised briefly on the lip and dived gracefully into the water.

Seconds later she reappeared, thrashing towards, the bank, an expression of sheer astonishment on her face. "This water..." she cried incredulously, "—it isn't wet!" She splashed a swathe of it into the air, where it sparkled like a skein of diamonds. "It just isn't wet..."

Soon the men joined her, sporting like excited children, whilst five spacesuits were left rapidly disintegrating on the rock. Jamieson's bottle of wine, freed from the shredded material, rolled with a faint plop into the pool, un-noticed. Weapons and collecting pouches softened and flowed like Dali watches, forming irregular treacly puddles, which slowly evaporated, leaving no trace on the pale stone. Sunlight continued to filter down through the stiff leaves of the hollow-fruit trees onto the rippling water. Bell-birds called in the distance.

At length the crew of *Beaumaris Castle* emerged, perfectly dry yet strangely refreshed, to bask at the water's edge. Their suits had entirely vanished. Without a backward glance, the five naked astronauts began to ascend the steep slope to the plain.

As they climbed, Margaret Thurnam noticed a strange opalescent sheen where the dappled sunlight bathed their skin. They gradually emerged above the tree-line and she noticed, with curiosity rather than horror, that she could dimly discern tufts of apple-moss through the flesh of their feet. She held up a hand, and discovered that some trick of the light made it appear translucent. She glanced at her companions. Their naked bodies had taken on the appearance of straw-coloured jelly, through which their bones showing through faintly, like underexposed x-ray plates.

Undismayed, the skeletons, becoming fainter with each unrecorded moment, strode forward, arm in arm, towards the crumpled remains of the ship. As they watched, it slumped to the ground and collapsed like a slowly deflating balloon.

Five faint shadows sat by the cluster of strange flowers that had sprung up amongst the blackened remains of the Survey-ship *Beaumaris Castle*.

The insubstantial forms basked a little longer in the timeless sunset, then were gone....

Exclusive!

PLAYPERSON Magazine   14th May 2033

Sitting here in my cramped quarters aboard *Delver*, so many light-years from Mother Earth, it is poignant to leaf through the two well-thumbed recipe books I have been permitted to bring with me in my capacity as Head Cook and Bottle Steriliser. Poignant, since shipboard ingredients are so very unimaginative and cooking facilities so inadequate for anything beyond basic starship fare. Even our "wines" consist of various coloured powders, which are added to recycled water. At times I come close to despair.

I am assured that the planet and its teeming life-forms have already been described in some detail in news-cassettes and considerable footage shown on world-wide tri-vision. I will therefore merely remind readers that our expedition landed—none too softly, I fear,—to plant the flag of the United World Federation on Xebulon's highest mountain. This we have provisionally named Mount Ebanks, in memory of our gallant Captain, Sir Edmund Banks, who, shortly after our arrival, had the misfortune to be devoured by a carnivorous marsh-bear.

An orbital survey made before our somewhat precipitate descent, has yielded accurate maps of the terrain around us. These are proving invaluable to the parties of Zeno-biologists, Geologists, Archaeologists and other specialists, who, even now, are investigating the unparalleled resources which surround us, and are attempting to elucidate the many mysteries of this curious planet. It seems that the once-dominant life-form, a sentient, three-foot tall creature whose skeletal remains are strikingly reminiscent of a six-armed chimpanzee, died out many centuries ago, for reasons which still elude us. They left behind a wealth of artefacts, which have been eagerly collected and are currently being investigated by our team of experts. Little did I think, when I first embarked upon *Delver*, that I would be called upon, in my own humble capacity as cook, to make a positive contribution to our understanding of an alien culture. Strange are the ways of fate! Had not Lee Wong, the cook originally selected for the expedition, broken his leg a few hours before takeoff, I would not have had the honour of examining in some detail one of the most startling finds of the expedition. This is nothing less than a primitive form of cookery book, dated by the radio-carbon method to no less than 2,530 earth-years ago.

Our linguists and cryptographers have worked unremittingly at the task of elucidating the spidery hand-written text, penned by some unknown Xebulonic Escoffier over two and a half millennia ago! Particular tribute must be paid to Johnson, our philologist—a man endowed with a droll sense of humour, who often amuses us with his risible anecdotes in times of depression. Of which there are many. His practical jokes occasionally cause friction amongst those whose own sense of humour has perhaps become a little blunted by our tribulations. However, my own spirits are high, and should I ever become the butt of one of his japes, I trust I will bear it with more fortitude than poor Visconsi...

Johnson is an excellent fellow at heart, and it was he who made the vital breakthrough in translating the curious script of this remarkable creature, thereby enabling me to transmit the text of one of these unique recipes. I long for the opportunity to try it myself, but sadly, for logistical and practical reasons, this is not yet practicable. I am constrained by the paucity of basic ships stores, and by the inadequacies both of the on-board microwave cookers and the primitive barbeque I have constructed outdoors. The now superfluous space-helmets, even when fitted with handles, I find, make but poor substitutes for good old-fashioned pots and pans...

Three chivalrous members of our crew, on learning that curried noodles were to form the basis of the fifth consecutive meal, volunteered to sample various luscious-looking fruits found in abundance in this region. Their funeral service, a sombre affair, naturally, was conducted with full military honours. Their passing serves as a sad and sobering object lesson to those of us who remain. Regretfully, therefore, my offer to prepare a lavish banquet from the mouth-wateringly succulent life-forms around us has been postponed pending full toxicological investigations. Once these teething problems have been overcome, we look forward to dining in style, here on this beautiful, bountiful planet upon which we have (to put it bluntly) crashed. Somewhat disastrously.

However, I fear I have digressed from the purpose of my missive, which is to lay before readers of *Playperson* Johnson's inspired translation of recipe number 42 from Unthang's Illustrated Book of

Cookery, to which I have appended some comments which I hope will be of some value. It should be unnecessary to stress that our suggested earth-equivalents (or substitutes for) ingredients, quantities, cooking-times etc., are provisional only and in the light of future research, may be open to alternative interpretations. Despite these caveats, I have every confidence that the recipe I offer will prove worthy to grace the table of any family back there on distant Earth. To which, alas, we can never return, judging by the parlous condition of the shattered hulk which was once the proud starship *Delver*.

PLEASE NOTE—Xebulon's water supply is very rich in minerals and trace elements. Chemical analysis suggests that the nearest equivalent is probably Spa Water from Buxton, England. However, any bitter-tasting natural spring water will probably serve.

Unthang's Recipe
(translated by Johnson, notes by Fancy, 2032)

Literal Translation	Fancy's Notes
Gumph Casserole	(Steak?) Casserole
Serves 17	6 humans (estimated)
Wavicles:—	Ingredients:—
9-10 pockles, backside of gumph	Try 3 - 3.5 lb. rump steak
2 Yig of Phip	4 tablespoons (beef dripping?)
Half a Yig of Flarg	1 tbs. (ground chalk?) substitute flour?
3 Gllomms Grimp	5 pints water (see note above)
4 Pupples	Kind of soft fruit ? Try tomatoes

(continued)

Unthang's Recipe (continued)

4 large sliced Plaths   Type of fungus.
                                        Mushrooms should
                                        be OK

.5 Yig of Ook   1 tbs. butter (Johnson
                                        says treacle)

Pinch of Sparle   Pepper, to taste

<u>Method</u>: Marinade the meat for at least 36 Poings (approximately
         12 hours) in a mixture of *(Continued on page 234)*

New To Science...

Malchin bid his host goodnight and, pulling his thick coat tightly around himself, left the timber-framed cottage. The door was closed firmly behind him against the keen wind, which bit like acid.

He walked down the steep road with exaggerated care, holding himself erect and placing each foot on the ground with great deliberation. His controlled movements were intended to mask the fact that he had imbibed a little too freely of Paulk's Slivovitz. As he rounded the corner he started to giggle. His studded boots rang on the rough cobbles of the road, yet it appeared to him that his feet did not quite make contact with the ground. He was floating, surely? It was a curious, but not unpleasant sensation, and a bubble of laughter escaped his lips. He pulled himself together and continued down the hill.

Had he not been so preoccupied guiding his errant feet towards his own cottage he might have observed more closely the strange manifestation taking place far above him in the star-peppered sky. A small globe, intensely blue in colour, was pulsating regularly, immobile against the black velvet heavens. It had been clearly visible for some minutes before Malchin glanced in that direction. A streak of white light leaped from the ball and arced downwards, to land somewhere beyond the belt of trees which shielded Pandim's Garden from the prevailing wind. The blue sphere vanished.

"Shooting star," Malchin muttered thickly and hiccupped.

He remembered nothing more of the previous evening when he woke to find sunlight streaming onto his bed. The incident of the shooting star merged with his dull recollections of an evening spent with Paulk, playing chess and putting the world to rights. He dressed as rapidly as he was able before going downstairs to make himself a generous mug of pungent Turkish coffee.

A few minutes later he left the cottage and hurried to Pandim's

Garden, the main tourist attraction of this remote Yugoslavian village. The garden had been created over seventy years earlier by the region's most famous botanist. A renowned climber, Pandim had gathered together an unrivalled collection of local plants, culled from inaccessible ledges high in the mountains that enclosed the village as if in the palm of a clawed hand. After his retirement as Professor of Botany at some unbelievably remote university, he had returned to the place of his birth and had devoted the remainder of his long life to expanding his unique collection.

Malchin, a good field botanist and gifted gardener, had taken on responsibility for the collection nearly twenty years ago, and was now a significant figure in the local economy. In addition to maintaining the garden, he had in recent years become responsible for showing round coach-loads of tourists who were increasingly drawn to the wild beauty of the region. The modest admission charge, together with the sale of rare plants which he assiduously propagated in the frame-yard, and the income from refreshments, craft-work and souvenirs sold in the village, Pandim's Garden yielded a modest but very welcome contribution to the prosperity of the area. If their prized purchases were confiscated by the customs officials, that was not Malchin's problem.

As he produced the key to unlock the wrought iron gate by the kiosk, he heard the distant sound of a coach which, in low gear, was winding its way up the zigzag road. He had made it just in time. He opened the kiosk, propped open its window and laid out the illustrated souvenir booklets (with captions in several languages), the selection of post cards and CDs. Finally he opened the great ledger in which he scrupulously recorded his takings, and laid his pen on the counter beside it.

Soon the tourists—an English party on this occasion—were progressing in all directions along the carefully laid slabs which formed the pathways, examining the remarkable collection with 'oohs' and 'aahs' of enthusiasm as they discovered unfamiliar species. The true connoisseurs were easily detected, for it was they who passed the more spectacular, showy plants with a cursory nod, and went into raptures over some insignificant little growth culled from a remote crevice amongst the peaks.

Malchin had quickly discovered that it was impractical to herd parties along the maze of paths. They preferred to hunt in small groups of perhaps three or four, which progressed at different rates. He had a rudimentary grasp of several European languages, and during each visit he covered a good deal of ground, speaking briefly to the various groups, answering their questions as best he could.

One of these parties, consisting of two men, three women and a youth, was clustered around a large boulder near the highest point of the steeply-sloping garden. Their discussion was becoming heated as Malchin came within earshot. They looked up as he took a short cut across some stepping-stones over a shallow pool to reach them.

"Perhaps you could settle an argument for us," one of the men began.

Malchin looked at him, uncomprehending. He spread his hands and smiled apologetically.

"What...is...this...plant?" the man demanded slowly and loudly, pointing to something on top of the rock.

Malchin stared at the thing in astonishment. He had never seen any plant even remotely like it before. Yet its form seemed vaguely familiar. With a thrill of excitement he realised that it resembled a picture he had once seen in a book, what was it now? Ah, yes! A crinoid—that was it. A deep-sea creature like a starfish on the end of a long, segmented stalk. But—a crinoid could not possibly survive out of water, and what could it be doing here, in Pandim's garden?

It waved slightly in the breeze, its feathery arms scintillating in improbable shades of mauve and blue, tiny flecks of bright crimson flickering on and off as they caught the sunlight. Its two-foot long stalk was a chestnut colour. Surely crinoids—"Sea Lilies", that was their common name, displayed no such lavish decoration? It was a plant of exceptional beauty—quite exquisite and unique in form...

He hated to lose face by admitting that the thing was an utter mystery to him—that he had not the vaguest idea of what it could be, or how it came to be there. The coach driver had introduced him proudly as "Curator of the famous Pandim plant collection—acknowledged authority on the plants of Yugoslavia". The man had laid it on a bit thick—he always did—but Malchin felt that his professional integrity was now at stake and he had no desire to be dismissed as a charlatan.

"Exceptional plant" he began, trying to formulate a plausible reply that was as close to the truth as he could make it. "Newly discovered, here in Pandim's famous garden. New to science, it is thought. You are the first visitors to see it. In a class of its own. No name yet".

Sensing the excitement, other parties made their way up the slope to view the wonderful new plant. All agreed that it was quite the most remarkable and beautiful thing they had ever seen. Several of them demanded to buy seed from it, but he was compelled to disappoint them. "No seed yet. But you may photograph, for a small fee."

He stood guard over the plant until the last tourist was leaving the garden. His pockets stuffed with coins and banknotes, he followed them down to the entrance. At the kiosk stood a tall grey-haired gentleman, who took him aside, slipping an address card into his hand.

"Look", he said, with a furtive glance over his shoulder "a friend of mine, he nursery-man—nursery-man, *compredez*?" Malchin nodded. "Give anything you like for a cutting, or a seedling,—whatever. Just name your price. Contact me at this address. Sure we can come to terms." He rubbed his thumb and forefinger together and winked knowingly.

Malchin waved the coach away, went into the kiosk and entered the amount he had taken in photographic fees, entering them as gratuities. He was a punctiliously honest man. Then he locked the gate and fastened to it a cardboard placard which proclaimed "Regrets, Garden she Close" in a selection of European languages. He had to have time to think...

That afternoon he roped off the path leading to the top of the garden and erected some wattle screens around the rock. Armed with a selection of botanical reference books, he attempted, with little hope of success, to discover what the strange plant could be.

He worked systematically through each of the books, but the strange plant was so distinctive, and so devoid of normal characteristics used in identification, that his efforts were futile. He realised that he would have to consult some higher authority. Its five feathery "leaves"— appendages might be a more appropriate term—were moving slowly, quite independently of each other. No movements of the air could account for their seemingly purposeful activity. He was reminded, vaguely of the movements of a sequence of semaphore signals. Flags that changed colour, and flashed with intermittent spots of crimson light. The effect was almost hypnotic, and his head began to spin. With a groan, he cursed Paulk and his confounded Slivovitz! Why, for a moment he had almost convinced himself that the thing had been trying to signal to him!

He pulled himself together, laid aside his useless books and tried to reason the thing out. The strange plant was entirely outside the scope of his knowledge. It could be some freak of nature—a unique genetic mutation, or, much more likely, it was something exotic. After all, pollen and seeds were often found floating in the upper atmosphere, and could travel immense distances in this way. It could have come from the Andes, the Himalayas—anywhere. He would have to consult someone familiar with the flora of other lands. At length his mind was made up.

Cautiously he attempted to remove one of its curious, fleshy 'petals'. As his fingers came into contact with it, a searing pain ran up his arm. It was like a powerful electric shock and he was flung backwards against the screen. He picked himself up, more astonished than hurt, and put on his heavy gardening gloves. This gave him a measure of protection as he attempted to wrench the petal free.

It might have been made of steel! Eventually he was able to cut it off with the aid of secateurs, and was most disappointed to observe that its bright coloration disappeared immediately, almost as if he had switched off the lights on a Christmas tree. With a shrug he sandwiched the specimen between two stout pieces of cardboard, wrote a detailed covering letter and arranged for it to be posted off to the current Professor of Botany at Pandim's old university. Then he took out the English tourist's calling card and fingered it thoughtfully.

· · · · · ·

He spent every minute of his spare time during the next few days searching for further specimens of the plant, which, if it were truly new to science, he had respectfully requested might be called "*Pandimium malchinianum*", thus commemorating his own name alongside that of the great Pandim. His search was fruitless, but he felt it was only a matter of time. After all, the plant had to have come from somewhere.

It was almost a fortnight after he had posted the letter that the reply reached him. Professor Boehm was brief and to the point. He was convinced that the specimen represented a form of life hitherto unknown, and which displayed many very peculiar properties. It was neither plant nor animal, and its chemistry was so utterly unlike anything known to science that the organism might have a non-terrestrial origin. Malchin was to make sure that no-one tampered with it in any way, and to guard it with his life until the university party arrived. They were almost ready to depart.

Malchin groaned. It was two days since he had carefully, and with great difficulty, sacrificed the thing to make seven cuttings, which were now in the propagating frame. They looked dull and lifeless. Too late he realised that he should have been patient, and waited for it to flower... *If it ever would have flowered, of course.*

The Private Viewing

Howard Wilkes slumped untidily in the swivel chair by his desk and proceeded to wallow in his own misfortunes. This was the only masochistic pleasure left to him from his tenure of the Templeton Gallery. An elegant china cup of coffee, long since grown cold, stood by his elbow. It was Monday, and felt like it.

The white-painted walls were bare. At the end of the previous week the last artist had wandered dejectedly from the gallery bearing his final pitiful bundle of badly-framed daubs which had so lamentably, and so understandably, failed to sell. Wilkes had warned him about the frames from the start. "I can't afford seventy or eighty quid a time!" the straggly-bearded art student had protested. "The frames would cost more than I'm asking for the pictures! These are just temporary. Whoever buys them can get proper frames made to their own taste." Wilkes' view that the frame was part of the composition was rejected, and the pictures hung in their "temporary" frames; and had not sold.

Wilkes' receptionist, Penny, with scarcely a backward glance, had followed the artist out, a macramé hand-bag dangling loosely from her shoulder. In addition to her final pay-packet, he presented her with a small trinket from his unsold stock—a tawdry souvenir of her brief period of service at the gallery.

A "Closed" sign hung askew at the plate-glass entrance doors, an angry bluebottle buzzing aimlessly around it.

At length Wilkes stirred, lit a rather stale cheap cigar and pondered. His lease on the building was renewable some seven weeks hence, but he knew he could not face another year of failing to sell incompetent daubs to an indifferent public. The venture had commenced with great enthusiasm, and the gallery's receipts had shown a most encouraging buoyancy. Indeed, for over two years he had generated a modest but steady profit, after paying the wages of his secretary, a part-time cleaner and an odd-job man paid by the hour. After the very profitable Janet Bowker exhibition, there had been a steady decline, and Penny had finally been paid off, leaving him to reflect upon his misfortunes and wind up the affairs of the gallery.

In the early days he could confidently expect to sell around a third of the various works exhibited in each show. Then, attendances had begun to fall, along with sales. So, too, he acknowledged, had the quality of his exhibitions. He seemed to have exhausted the supply of local artistic talent. The recent show of sculptures by Charles Thompson had been a complete farce, and he shuddered at the recollection.

The most hateful aspect of the whole thing was that he had been forced to demean himself before his dwindling clientele by his rapturous, if inscrutable, comments on the strange and ill-assorted assemblages of paintings that adorned, if that was the word, the walls of his gallery. Works vapid and insipid, facile and futile, works virile and puerile—all were grist to his mill.

He glowed, he enthused, as he deployed his threadbare platoon of clichés under the bright banner of "significance". Drawings were by turn "taut; brief; evocative; introspective." Occasionally they might be "powerful". Water-colours called up the light infantry of his vocabulary, and were often "Witty". Oils and acrylics brought his light cavalry into the fray—"Inner tension; ethereal quality of chiaroscuro; sombre restraint; extrovert ebullience..." Abstracts demanded no less than a direct bombardment from his heavy artillery—"Inner tension; paradoxical ambivalence; idiosyncratic perception." One of his favourite (and least comprehensible) expressions was "Contrapuntal iconoclasm", which he sometimes modified into "Iconoclastic contrapuntalism". Not that it made a scrap of difference to his shell-shocked visitors, who, afraid to reveal their ignorance, sought refuge back amongst the drawings, or made a strategic retreat to the exit. Just occasionally, vanquished by his eloquence, or merely in self-defence, one of his victims would slowly take out his cheque-book.

At least, Wilkes consoled himself, he had never been guilty of simpering cajolery; his sales pitch had been a spirited defence of the indefensible. He sighed. Where had real artistic talent gone? The incredible diversity of the works he had exhibited served to mask the features they had in common—a lack of genuine commitment, inspiration and self-discipline. Perhaps this was a reflection of the times; perhaps artists were...

Wilkes' maudlin reflections were abruptly shattered by an imperious ring from the doorbell. He rose from his seat, brushing cigar ash from his ample waistcoat, and ambled to the door. Outside stood an imposing figure in a smart beige trench coat. The man was tall and slender, with a sallow face and a neat Van Dyke beard; but it was his eyes which immediately seized Wilkes' attention. They were unbearably piercing, and in their black depths minute flecks of gold seemed to scintillate like points of fire.

It was several seconds before Wilkes could tear his gaze away from this striking face and unfasten the door. "Mr. Wilkes," said the stranger in a sonorous voice. It was a statement rather than a question.

"Why, yes. How may I help you?"

The tall man gestured towards the office. "May we...?"

"Of course. Do come in, Mr. ...?"

There was no reply. Instead, the tall figure entered and strode confidently into Wilkes' inner sanctum, where, unbidden, he drew a chair to the side of the desk and sat down. A little taken aback, Wilkes mustered his dignity and took his seat, looking quizzically at his visitor. There was a prolonged silence.

"Mr. Wilkes, your gallery is closed. It is likely to remain so, I understand. Your credit is, shall we say, problematic, your recent exhibitions having met with little success."

The proprietor's fists tightened, unseen below the level of the desk. He half rose, indignant that a total stranger, who had made no appointment, should seek to humiliate him in this way.

"Do not mistake my intent, Mr. Wilkes. I have no wish to humiliate you. I merely wish to verify certain facts. Indeed, I have every sympathy. Every sympathy." The voice was cultivated and bore a faint, unfamiliar accent. East European, perhaps?

"Tell me, Mr. Wilkes, what are your future plans—your aspirations?"

"I've been trying to avoid thinking about that for some time."

"But I respectfully suggest that you must, Mr. Wilkes. Indeed you must. At this time you have little alternative but to look to your future. The dole queues are long, and your qualifications are—how shall I put this—a little sparse."

Wilkes unconsciously crumpled a matchbox to pulp as he took a deep breath. This self-assured, overbearing stranger was deliberately adding insult to humiliation!

"I have no desire to insult you, Mr. Wilkes, I am intrigued. Please bear with me. Now, I would like you to daydream a little... Tell me, what do you most desire? No, allow me to re-phrase my question. You have enjoyed some modest success in the past; at present your existence is... precarious. As to the future, well, who knows?" He smiled bleakly and spread his enormous hands, palms upward, above the desk. "What future do you see for yourself? What future can you reasonably anticipate in present circumstances? More to the point, Mr. Wilkes, what future would you create for yourself, were such a thing within your power?" The piercing eyes met his and held them, unblinking.

"Well," began Wilkes uncertainly, " I would like to make a real success of this gallery. I've put a lot of effort into it, and I feel I have somehow been let down."

"Success, Mr. Wilkes; what is success? Do you mean that you would wish to extend your lease and continue to make a precarious living by selling mediocrity to the gullible? Would that constitute success?"

"No, I aspire to more than that. I would like to stage a really outstanding exhibition—better than anything I have yet produced: something that would really make the Arts Council sit up and take notice!"

"Ah! The Arts Council... I believe they were forced to discontinue their meagre contribution to your project a couple of years ago. What vaunting ambition, Mr. Wilkes! But surely this gallery is too small to stage anything capable of renewing the interest of that august body. Would you not prefer to take charge of the National Gallery, say, or the Tate?" His tone was faintly mocking, but Wilkes chose to ignore the jibe.

"Since we are dealing in abstractions, no! Those establishments are national institutions. They exist, they are paid for from the taxes we are compelled to pay. Their directors merely preserve and maintain them, making small improvements here and there, or spectacular ones if they are favoured by the lottery people. This little gallery, on the other hand, is my world. I created it from a derelict carpet shop. From cellar to attic it is my work, and mine alone. I converted it, rewired it, clad the walls, installed cases, carpets and decor."

"A moment ago you said that you felt 'let down'. By whom were you 'let down'?"

"By the artists themselves! We staged splendid shows at first, but real talent seems to have dried up. Once upon a time artists had wealthy patrons—the aristocracy, rich merchants, the Church. The artist was a wage-slave, yet somehow he was able to create masterpieces to order. In such circumstances, one might expect nothing but hack-work. Nowadays artists have complete freedom; surely we have the right to expect some quite outstanding work to result from this freedom?"

"Mr. Wilkes, I asked you to day-dream." He smiled benignly. "But let us be clear; most of the paintings produced for those old-time patrons was in truth pure hack-work. Time, thankfully, has eradicated much, but by no means all of the trivia, much of which still holds pride of place in galleries and private collections throughout the world. That a number, a very small number, of *really* great works should have been produced in such circumstances was inevitable.

"As to the present—well, artists have freedom, indeed! Freedom to starve, freedom to prostitute their talents for ready cash, freedom to fulminate against society, freedom to break with tradition—to trample convention under foot. Iconoclasm can be a very necessary thing, but with what will that which was destroyed be replaced? Is the Arts Council, to take your point, as good a judge of the art of this age as were, say, the Medici, in theirs? Some of this contemporary art, a minute fraction of one percent, is worthy of preservation; but this is scarcely significant—the percentage always *was* minuscule, Mr. Wilkes.

"Today, officially commissioned works are relatively few, and of these, all too high a proportion consist of portraits of nonentities who will ultimately be consigned to the limbo of history. Of the vast output of works no so commissioned, the majority are speculative works, designed to appeal to the lowest common denominator of popular taste and offered for sale in venues such as this..." he waved airily round the gallery, "which goes some way to explaining the occasionally remunerative shows you have featured. Other works, not usually quite so crass, by and large, are created by the artist for his own satisfaction. Sadly, such artists tend to be easily satisfied, and are content to wallow like pigs in their own mire.

"But just occasionally, Mr. Wilkes, a flash of genius lights up this dismal scene. It strikes where it will—from the Royal Academician to the penniless artist in his garret or the child daubing poster paint on cardboard. Almost invariably such flashes are unobserved or unremarked; they vanish without trace and without regret. At this very moment an artist on this little planet may be at work on a masterpiece. The chances are overwhelmingly against it being recognised as such, and the prospect of it outliving its creator are remote indeed.

"In this very gallery, Mr. Wilkes, you yourself have exhibited some seven pictures which may be described as good, one remarkably fine piece of sculpture, and—no less than three masterpieces! This is a quite remarkable achievement, and I salute your perspicacity, if such it be." The man leaned forward over the desk and looked directly into the eyes of the gallery owner. "Art is a strange business, Mr. Wilkes, a strange business altogether. Dream again, but give your dreams the freedom you value so highly."

With an immense effort, Wilkes restrained his temptation to strike the mocking face before him. His body slumped like a punctured tyre as he considered. At length he had his answer. "Then I want to stage an exhibition of masterpieces only. Just one last exhibition, but everything in it must be, simply, the best."

"I fear you are incapable of recognising a masterpiece when you see one; the last which passed through your hands you sold for seventy-five pounds, including the frame. Another was not sold, and the artist painted over it shortly after he collected it from you. You can judge competence, Mr. Wilkes, but even you cannot recognise genius."

"I've only your word for that," snapped Wilkes, roused at last. "Who are you, anyway? And what do you want with me? I've a good mind to fling you out on your ear!"

"Calm yourself," the man said with a good-natured laugh. "I am merely teasing—toying with semantics. I have just intimated that masterpieces are excessively rare, and yet from another standpoint they are as common as blades of grass."

Wilkes rose from his seat again, bristling with indignation. "What on earth do you mean?" he demanded. "You are talking in riddles. Are you here simply to waste my time, or are you deliberately provoking me?"

"Is time such a precious commodity to you at this juncture, then?" he asked archly, fixing Wilkes again with those penetrating eyes. "No, my friend, my time is too valuable to me to waste it. This is no idle conversation, although I am playing with words just to draw you out."

"Perhaps you would be so kind as to explain what you mean, then, by saying that masterpieces are both extremely rare, yet commonplace? I think you are a fraud, or a lunatic, sir !"

"A paradox, is it not? But consider the following proposition, and consider it well; the best a person is capable of doing may be regarded as his own personal masterpiece. It may consist of applying various patches of paint to a canvas, but it is much more likely to be something less pretentious. The writing of a letter to an aged aunt, one specific act of making love to a beautiful woman, the cooking of a perfect soufflé, the achievement of a flawless drive on the golf course; even the digging of an immaculate ditch. And, of course, each masterpiece must be considered in relation to its creator's limitations. Each day every person is creating a masterpiece, or a series of them, *within his limitations at the time*. In the final analysis, every action, every thought may be regarded as a masterpiece in the given circumstances. No-one ever lost a hundred yards race, nor a marathon, for that matter, if the precise handicap of each competitor were correctly allowed for."

"Ah, but there is another criterion—surely *effort* made must distinguish the winner..."

"Not even that! The fact that one runner has more motivation than another must also be taken into account in the handicapping procedure. So you see, from this standpoint, the very word 'masterpiece' becomes meaningless."

"We are still playing games!"

"Of course we are. I merely wish to suggest that the concept of a masterpiece is in some ways a mirage. It may mean much, or nothing at all. Almost invariably we use the term to signify an achievement so remarkable that it transcends time, becoming a sort of universal verity. But consider yet again—does not fashion also enter into our judgment? How many plays and novels once hailed as unrivalled are now un-played, unread, totally disregarded? How many Victorian canvasses by accomplished academicians, once given pride of place in public galleries now languish unseen in the cellars? Occasionally such anachronisms are hauled from the depths to feature briefly, in some temporary exhibition, to be gazed upon for a time. But all too often, the vital spark seems to have been extinguished by time, and these quaint fossils are returned, shrouded, to their crypts."

"Yet another common human failing," he continued, is to confuse rarity with value. The Ancient Greeks produced good competent pieces of statuary by the thousand, but I assure you that barely a handful of those which survive would have been regarded as anything out of the ordinary at the time of their creation. Yet every one which has been unearthed in a fair state of preservation in recent times has been hailed as triumphant proof of the genius of the Golden Age, and pensioned off to some museum of fine art, or the patio of some millionaire."

"But..."

"I know, Mr. Wilkes; they are interesting relics, and a surprisingly large number of them are good. Which are true masterpieces, in our more restricted meaning of the word, I will not divulge."

"You know, of course! " Wilkes exploded indignantly. "I had not realised that you are an authority—I'm terribly sorry," he added, his voice heavy with sarcasm, "*The* authority on Greek statuary!"

"As a matter of fact, yes, amongst many other things. But this is not necessarily to say that my knowledge accords with the opinions of our contemporary 'experts'. In point of fact, it rarely does. You see, Mr. Wilkes, I can produce for you as many masterpieces for you as you like. I can even inculcate in you the appreciation of a masterpiece when it is placed before you."

"I've had just about enough of this. You arrive unbidden; you insult me to my face; you ramble on about art, pretending you know it all; indulge in metaphysical nonsense; then you have the gall to announce that you can produce masterpieces out of a hat! I must now ask you to leave, whoever you are—you haven't even had the courtesy to give me your name. Not that I particularly want it now that I have discovered that you are either a charlatan or a lunatic. Now, kindly get out of my gallery!"

The stranger smiled benignly. "Anger, Mr. Wilkes. Righteous and understandable indignation! I really must apologise for my conduct. But now we come to the crucial point—would you care to examine a masterpiece for yourself?"

"So finally we reach the truth," jibed Wilkes, "you are a salesman! I should have realised it as soon as I saw you."

Those piercing eyes transfixed him again. "Kindly pass me that scrap of paper from the top of your filing cabinet. And a pencil, if you please. A sharp one."

Perplexed, Wilkes did as requested and waited, a mocking expression on his face.

"Witness now, the creation of a masterpiece!"

The man's hand held the pencil motionless above the paper for perhaps three seconds. Then, with a furious onslaught, he scribbled back and forth across the sheet, his hand an insubstantial blur against the white of the paper. Seconds later he stopped and pushed it over the polished desk to Wilkes, who stared at it in blank astonishment. Before him lay the most astounding drawing he had ever seen! It depicted a huge statue set in a town square lined with unfamiliar, stunted trees. Scores of robed figures surrounded the plinth of the statue, where a mason was inscribing a row of letters. The amount of detail was staggering, but perhaps even more astonishing was the way in which the textures of the various materials, stone, leaves, clouds, cloth, were represented. Much clearer than any photograph, this pencil sketch appeared to be a miniature fragment of Time, the figures temporarily frozen, the leaves stilled, to allow close examination.

Wilkes, holding the precious piece of paper in tremulous fingers, sagged back in his chair, utterly speechless. There was a pregnant silence.

Eventually his visitor coughed politely. Wilkes replaced the paper on his desk, remarking weakly that he needed a drink. Going over to the filing cabinet, he opened the bottom drawer, from which he withdrew first a bottle of sherry and a smaller one of whiskey and two finger-marked glasses. "Would you care ..." he invited, proffering one of the glasses.

"Most kind. Yes, perhaps I will join you in a small Scotch."

Wilkes poured. "Your very good health, my friend," smiled the stranger, raising his glass. Wilkes mumbled an incomprehensible reply before gulping down the raw spirit and immediately refilling his glass.

"Look," he said at length, "this has to be some sort of trick. What you appeared to do is absolutely impossible. You must be a conjurer. Hah! Now I have it—you have hypnotised me. You have induced me to believe that you have made a wonderful drawing on this bit of paper. It's blank, really."

"I assure you, Mr. Wilkes, I have done no such thing! I will be leaving shortly and you may retain this trifle to examine at your leisure. It's real enough, I assure you, and it wasn't a conjuring trick. There's an eraser in your desk—it will rub out quite easily; it really is a pencil sketch."

"But... I simply do not understand. It's the most incredible thing I ever witnessed. It's...it's a masterpiece!"

"Congratulations, Mr. Wilkes, for the first time, you have actually recognised one."

"Just who are you? What is your name? Where were you trained? Why have you come to me, when your talent..."

"One question at a time, Mr. Wilkes, I implore!" chuckled the man, his face puckered in merriment. Some time ago I asked you a question. You have had ample time to consider your reply. In the light of our conversation, pray tell me what, specifically, do you most desire for the future?

He replied without hesitation. "It's quite obvious, now, more than anything, I want to stage a one-man show of your drawings. Right here, in this gallery. Before the lease expires. It would be a sensation!"

The man nodded. "It would indeed."

Faced with sudden misgivings, Wilkes dropped his voice with embarrassment. "Er... I hate to ask this, but what sort of price do you ask for your works? You see, we,—the gallery, that is—normally..."

"You want your commission!" he chortled. "Naturally. Charge whatever you think fit. I won't haggle. But why do you wish to confine the showing merely to drawings? After all, it's a somewhat limited medium. Wouldn't you are to exhibit some of my oils? A few watercolours—some sculptures. Wall-hangings, perhaps?"

Wilkes, in the act of swallowing his third glass of neat whiskey spluttered. "You mean you produce work of this quality in other media, too?"

"Anything you like."

"Would you have sufficient works to fill this gallery? Soon?"

"I can fill your gallery, and then some!" Glancing at his watch, he added quickly. "I seem to have stayed somewhat longer than I anticipated. It has been a most stimulating conversation, but I'm afraid I have another appointment shortly."

"Not with... some other gallery!" wailed Wilkes.

"Nothing of that kind, Mr. Wilkes, Do calm yourself. You shall have exclusive rights to my works. But I really must be on my way."

"But the arrangements! We really must discuss the arrangements. I mean, posters, catalogues, a Private Viewing, the media to contact, invitation cards, refreshments, insurance and so on..."

"I simply do not have time to go into all that at present. I'll tell you what—just lay on a couple of dozen bottles of wine. Good stuff, not the cheap 'plonk' you usually serve, mind! Leave everything else to me."

"But there just isn't time..."

"Time is no object—except that I must not be late for my next appointment. I'm a pretty fast worker, you know," he said with a wink and pointed to the drawing. "If it will make you feel easier, write down your name, address and telephone number in this little book of mine and I'll be in touch shortly. Here, use my fountain pen. Red ink, I'm afraid, but it will do."

"But your name?" Wilkes urged in desperation. "And where can I contact you?"

"All will be revealed in due course, Mr. Wilkes. I can assure you that your gallery will feature the most astounding collection of works of art ever assembled under one roof, and that you will retain the lease of this building until the end of your life. Now, I really must go. I promise I will do all that is necessary; just leave it all to me." With that he strode to the door and opened it. At last the trapped bluebottle escaped into the slightly polluted air of Great Templeton Street whilst Howard Wilkes locked the door again and settled at his desk, the bottle of whiskey in his hand.

During the next two days, Wilkes worked harder than he had ever done since the original opening of the gallery nearly six years previously. His financial position was so critical that he personally repainted the walls of both the ground floor and upper galleries. With a hired machine he shampooed the carpets. Old posters were removed from the notice board and he polished the plate glass of his showcases inside and out until they sparkled like new. From time to time he paused, and entered his now immaculate office to marvel afresh at the exquisite little drawing. Each time he gasped at its delicacy, its subtlety, its unbelievable intricacy. How he longed for the telephone to ring and to hear the voice of the stranger confirming their agreement.

The next morning the faint rattling of his letter-box sent him scurrying to collect the mail. No-one was in sight although the plate-glass double doors afforded a clear view in both directions along the street, and down Conran Drive which lay immediately across the road from the gallery. Yet there, on the tiles, lay a single post card. It had been delivered by hand; it bore no stamp. The writing was minute, but the calligraphy immaculate.

It read :

My Dear Mr. Wilkes,

This is to inform you that I shall call upon you next Tuesday morning with a comprehensive selection of my works.

The pictures are ready to hang and I will provide the necessary plinths for statuary and so on. I do hope you will have made arrangements for refreshments for the Private Viewing, which will take place that same evening. Don't forget the glasses, a detail which can so easily be overlooked. Sorry to leave you with this little chore, but you will appreciate that my time is somewhat limited at present. The food I will supply.

I shall be bringing several assistants to help with the staging of the exhibition, and I do hope you will welcome them to the reception - they will all have been working like demons on your behalf! Do not trouble yourself with invitations -

I have taken the liberty of doing all that is necessary on that score. Everyone who matters will be there and I can positively guarantee that there will be more than adequate coverage by the press.

I am sure that all concerned will enjoy a most entertaining evening together.

Yours in haste,

To Wilkes' chagrin, the signature consisted of an indecipherable scribble.

On the following Monday afternoon a firm of caterers delivered the wine and glasses. He placed the cardboard boxes in his office, then rang Penny, offering to reinstate her initially for a month, at a slightly higher salary. Unfortunately, he was informed, she had just gone away on a short holiday, but would contact him on her return.

That evening he retired to his compact flat in the attic above the upper gallery, but spent a restless night worrying about all the things that could go wrong. Above all, he was concerned that he might be the victim of an insane practical joke. Yet each time he peered at the little drawing, he knew that he had been in the presence of a genius, to whom all things seemed possible. At last he slept.

He was awakened by the insistent ringing of the relay bell above his bed. Scrambling into his clothes, he dashed down the two flights of stairs to the main entrance. He almost sobbed with relief as he saw the tall figure of the strange man. Under each arm he was carrying two large paper-wrapped parcels. Wilkes was simultaneously overjoyed and bitterly disappointed. The disappointment must have registered on his face as he unlocked the door.

"Good day to you, Mr. Wilkes. Don't be perturbed, this is but a small group of watercolours. My assistants will be along shortly with the bulk of the exhibits."

"Do come in," urged Wilkes, pushing back the two doors until their catches engaged. Taking one of the parcels, he ushered the man into the gallery.

"My word, you have been busy," said the man, looking appreciatively round the gallery.

"I've repainted the upper room, too, and I've set up tables for the wine and so on."

"Capital, capital! I congratulate you, Mr. Wilkes. This really is splendid."

"Please call me Howard."

"Of course. We shall be seeing a great deal of each other and working very closely together, Howard. You know, it's a little foible of mine, this anonymity. I like to draw the analogy of the 'Masked Wrestler'. You know—on television the publicity attracted by a mysterious wrestler who wears a rubber hood which completely covers his head, save for small apertures over his eyes, nose and mouth. In the absence of any real information, rumours abound; he is believed to hail from some exotic foreign clime, although in reality he may be a native of Bradford or Bristol. He's invariably a 'baddy', of course," he chuckled, "and he sports some outlandish nickname. Nick-name, now there's an inspiration—why not call me Nick?"

"That's very kind of you," murmured Howard, somewhat perplexed.

"Right then, Howard, perhaps you would be so kind as to open these parcels whilst I see where the others have got to."

Nick made his way to the door, leaving Howard quivering with excitement as he carefully unfastened the string. Then, closing his eyes, he removed the corrugated cardboard and took out the first picture, making sure that he held it glass uppermost. Tremulously he opened his eyes. He was awe-struck by the vision before him. A single orchid appeared to be protected by the glass. It was not a preserved, pressed specimen, but a perfect, living flower that cast its faint shadows against a background of pale buff. He stared at the slender frame, edge-on; the thing was impossible. It seemed that if he were to break the glass he could lift out the exotic flower and shake off the drops of water which glistened on its waxy petals. Eventually he laid it aside to examine the next picture.

This proved to be a seascape, the like of which he had never seen before. In a raging storm, a small sailing vessel was about to be dashed onto a vicious fang of rock that emerged from a tempestuous sea beneath a lowering sky. As he studied the minute detail, he felt an ungovernable fear rising in his throat. The incredibly minute faces of the doomed men registered the horror of their situation, poised on the brink of oblivion.

The picture almost slipped from his grasp. Thankfully, he put it down and turned to the next, which was an abstract composition in which geometrical and asymmetric forms were overlaid with clusters of varicoloured lines which seemed to protrude from the surface like free-standing rods of gold, green and purple. For an instant he seemed to be within it, a part of this ethereal concept, and understood for the first time, the inner meaning of an abstract painting. It was something beyond the power of words to express; its very existence defied explanation in other terms. Simply, it *WAS*.

The last picture in the first batch was a study of a fish, a deformed, sinister-looking creature which could exist only in the unlit depths of the ocean, or in the fertile imagination of a visionary genius. He turned to the other bundle, examining and marvelling afresh as he drew each new picture from its wrappings.

So engrossed was Howard Wilkes in his task that he was totally unaware of the arrival of Nick and his helpers

Four short, powerfully-built, swarthy men wearing dark overalls entered the gallery carrying a huge wooden packing crate. Placing it in the centre of the room, they left Nick to prise it open with a crowbar. The nerve-jangling screech of nails wrenched from timber did not impinge upon the gallery owner as he crouched before the representation of a complicated machine of unknowable function. Instinctively he knew it to depict something that existed, somewhere; or which would perhaps exist at some future time, or in some universe parallel to the one we inhabit...

Meanwhile, two further groups of helpers had gently eased two more gigantic crates through the double doors which were barely wide enough to accept them. Still more cases and bundles arrived and a small group of workers, now numbering perhaps twenty, were busily unpacking the contents and stacking them against the wall under the supervision of Nick.

Howard hurriedly placed down the last picture, which had almost caused him to vomit. It showed, in repulsive detail, the maggot-ridden corpse of a human being in the last stages of decay. Jolted back to reality, he turned in astonishment, observing for the first time the jostling crowd of figures who were now beginning to haul pictures and crates up the rather narrow staircase to the upper gallery. Behind him, rows of pictures rested against the walls and several unopened crates occupied the centre of the room. Over the hubbub he heard Nick's voice calling.

"Ah, Howard, I hope you don't mind, but I've taken it upon myself to decide that most of the sculptures would be best on the ground floor here. I'm just a little concerned about the strength of the joists above.

You've a touch of dry rot in that corner over there, by the way."

Howard surveyed the incredible scene around him as he sat, redundant, on the corner of a low wooden crate. It was simply beyond belief. Dark figures were perched on ladders, adjusting lights, snipping off lengths of stranded brass wire and constantly re-arranging a seemingly endless supply of pictures. Immediately opposite to where he sat, a colossal oil painting was being manhandled into position. It depicted in gruesome detail, two sets of gallows, from which the convulsed bodies of two condemned men who were writhing in the throes of death. Howard shuddered as Nick's cheery voice addressed him. "I do enjoy these hangings, Howard, don't you?" He laughed lightly at his own pun. Then his voice changed to one of concern. "I say, are you feeling all right? You look a little, well, distraught. Why don't you go and help yourself to a tot of whiskey?"

"I'm sorry, Nick. I feel a bit nauseous. I'll be better in a minute. I think I'll just slip outside for a breath of fresh air."

"I regret that will not be possible at the moment. Unfortunately my helpers have just stacked some crates in the entrance. The fire-door is blocked, too, for the nonce. We'll soon get it sorted out for you."

"But, Nick—don't you realise there are far too many works here? We can't possibly display all this—it would fill the Tate, at least!"

"You are quite right, as ever. But, if you will come with me to the upper gallery you'll find I've prepared a little surprise for you."

The upper floor was marginally less congested than the scene of chaos below. Threading his way between heaps of packaging, Nick led the way to the far end of the gallery. He stopped in front of a gigantic rectangular form standing against the wall and shrouded in white material.

Howard stared at the object in total disbelief. "How on earth did you get that thing up here? It's impossible to bring something that size up the stairs."

"Well, you know, Howard, someone once said 'There are more things in earth than your philosophy ever dreamed of'."

"In Heaven and earth; that was the quotation, I believe."

"Quite. Now, I'll give you the honour of unveiling this particular piece. I'm rather proud of it, if I do say so myself. Just pull that bit of string there."

Howard took a deep breath and tugged on the cord which hung to one side of the hidden picture. As the covering fell away, he gaped in utter astonishment. He appeared to be looking into another gallery beyond. It was a palatial apartment, illuminated by a row of great chandeliers, which diminished rapidly in size, the perspective indicating the enormous length of the room. It was without question, the most stunning *trompe-l'oeil* which could be conceived. The picture was unframed, its margins painted as perfect representations of generous moulded door jambs and architrave. The edge of the open door, with its heavy brass hinges, was clearly visible. Howard's jaw sagged open. Never, in his wildest imagination, could he have believed it possible to produce such a perfect illusion.

Nick's voice broke in. "I can see you are impressed. Most gratifying. I took a good deal of trouble over this—hours of work went into creating it. But you've not seen the half of it yet! Just watch this." He signalled to two of his assistants who were wheeling another large package through the gallery on a sack-truck. "In there with it; that's right." He indicated the doorway. The two figures promptly walked through the false opening. Howard watched as they passed into the picture, steadily diminishing in size as they proceeded along the left-hand wall, where they deposited their package on the rich maroon carpet. Then they turned and walked back towards the doorway, now increasing in size as they approached and reemerged from the *trompe l'oeil*.

It was at this point that Howard screamed. He pitched forward, slashing at the canvas with clawed hands. There was no resistance to his attack and he fell forwards into the fantastic room, where he lay whimpering on the floor.

"I did advise you to get yourself a drink, Howard," Nick said sympathetically as he entered. "Well, now that you are here, do get up and have a look at the room. This is where my very best pieces will be shown." Grasping Howard's arm in a vice-like grip, he raised the shaking figure to its feet, then producing a large can of paint and a decorator's brush, Nick rapidly painted out the doorway through which they had entered.

"You see, Howard, I'm afraid I cannot resist a little joke from time to time. What you saw from your own gallery was apparently a *trompe l'oeil*—but from where we now stand, this is the real world; at least, whilst we occupy it. And the beauty of it is that I can always paint in a new doorway, opening onto whatever I please. You know, I'm most grateful to you for inspiring this idea. I haven't had so much fun in aeons!"

Howard Wilkes, proprietor of the Templeton Gallery knew, now, that he was insane. It was the only explanation. At least that was the only explanation he could accept. The alternative was unthinkable: and yet...and yet...

"And yet, my dear Howard, you are still not quite sure," Nick laughed. "So disconcerting, isn't it? Still, better the Devil you know, that's what I always say!"

Howard's animal instinct urged him to flee. His intellect insisted that any attempt to escape was futile. In the event his body solved the dilemma; he collapsed in a crumpled heap on the deep pile of the carpet.

An incalculable length of time later, Wilkes stirred. He still lay where he had fallen in the sumptuous, yet windowless hall. Its walls were now crowded with Nick's paintings. Magnificent statues of all sizes and styles occupied the centre of the room, where they were interspersed with numerous display cases filled with priceless *objets d'art*. Of Nick and his workers there was no sign. The only sounds that pervaded the vast gallery were the ticking of a large clock and the crackling of a log fire which blazed in the ornately-carved marble fireplace. He rose unsteadily to his feet. There was something evil and oppressive in the atmosphere of that magnificent hall.

At the furthermost end he discerned an impressive pair of mahogany doors, which appeared to be the only exit. He moved slowly towards them, trying to avoid looking at Nick's creations, yet irresistibly drawn to gaze at several of them as he passed. Some, in elaborate gilded frames, were archaic in style—portraits, landscapes, allegorical scenes and other subjects entirely in keeping with the opulence of their surroundings. Mixed with these traditional works, yet somehow entirely appropriate, were "modern" works in austere contemporary frames. Cubist still-lifes, impressionist sunsets and pointillist street-scenes hung alongside pre-Raphaelite compositions. Disturbing surrealist visions vied for attention with Greek and Roman frescoes; Japanese prints contrasted with lascivious nudes. The gallery was a microcosm of artistic styles, periods and nationalities. He was frequently deflected from his course by incredible statues and showcases placed in strategic positions to exhibit their fabulous riches to perfection.

After what seemed an eternity he achieved his goal; the magnificent ormolu handles of the doors were within his reach. He stretched out his hand, but for an instant his nerve failed him—what if this doorway should prove to be yet another illusion, through which he might not pass without Nick's sanction. Or, infinitely more terrifying, were these the door to Hell itself?

He steeled his resolve and touched one of the handles. It was cold, hard and indubitably real. He paused, then grasping it firmly, thrust the lever downwards. He drew the door towards him until he revealed a chink of light. Peering through the slit he could see a magnificent hall, its walls clad in marble and adorned with semi-precious stones. Immediately before him lay a stone balustrade which spanned a broad balcony. The hall was deserted. With infinite caution he opened the door a little wider and eased himself through the aperture.

From each end of the balcony a stairway curved downwards into the colonnaded hall. He started to descend the stair to his left, lifting each foot in turn with infinite caution, and placing it on the tread below. He found he was taking the shallowest of breaths, yet he was terrified in case the whisper of air passing from his lungs should disturb the profound silence. The pounding of his heart in his chest must surely betray his presence.

Half way down, the twin staircases merged to form a landing, from which the double width stair led downwards to the chequered floor of the hall, facing another pair of ponderous doors. But Howard Wilkes did not see beyond the landing, for confronting him, at the foot of the right-hand flight, stood a superbly-wrought metal dragon, which arched its jointed neck towards him, baring its stainless-steel fangs and belching flames from its nostrils. He started to retreat, moving slowly backwards the way he had come. He glanced upwards and was horrified to discover that the balcony was now crowded with laughing faces, each raising a glass of wine towards him. Sound abruptly returned. At the head of the stair stood Nick, now clad in a close-fitting suit of crimson and carrying a trident. Small goat-like horns protruded from his forehead and a long tail twitched by his legs. His host of helpers, now dressed as demons, jostled behind him.

"Your very good health, Howard," said Nick, raising his glass. "Excellent wine, excellent. I compliment your taste. I do hope you are enjoying our little 'Private Viewing'. Most exhilarating. I thought it would be fun for us all to wear formal dress for the occasion. I've brought one for you. Here, catch..."

He tossed a small black parcel towards Wilkes. It unrolled itself as it fell, landing at his feet. It was a one-piece costume of black velvet upon which a skeleton was painted. With a yell of terror, he hauled himself onto the broad, sloping handrail and climbed over. As he clung to the polished stonework, afraid to drop into the darkness of the stairwell, Nick's gloating face appeared. "That's not the normal way out, Howard. In fact, there's no way out at all for you, I'm afraid." He flourished a small address book in his hand. "You really should have read the small print, you know."

Wilkes found his fingers slipping on the polished surface. He clutched desperately at one of the balusters, but his flailing hand missed and he felt himself falling; he crashed heavily onto the cold floor below. From above, the sound of raucous laughter and descending footsteps echoed round the great entrance hall as he searched frantically for some means of escape. Suddenly, when all seemed lost, he discovered a small door in one corner. He wrenched it open and found himself at the top of a narrow wooden stair. He rushed downwards, and nearing the bottom, he was astonished to see an open doorway. Beyond it was the familiar sight of Great Templeton Street, with cars, buses and pedestrians going about their business. He launched himself towards it. He crashed into the final, amazing *trompe l'oeil* painted on the wall of his own cellar.

Some days later the following brief notice appeared in one of the national newspapers; it was reported at much greater length in the locals:

DEATH OF ART GALLERY PROPRIETOR

A verdict of Accidental death was returned at the Coroner's Inquest last Friday following the death of Mr. Howard Sangster Wilkes (53), proprietor of the Templeton Gallery. His body, which was discovered by the owner of the premises, lay at the foot of a steep flight of steps in the basement of the building. Mr. Wilkes had sustained a broken neck, the result of a heavy fall. There were no suspicious circumstances.

The completely empty gallery, which had been in financial difficulties for some time, is to be redeveloped as a night club...

Manuscript Found on a Computer

"**I**S ANYBODY THERE?"

"Madam Blavansky," known to confidantes as Madge Butterworth, spinster, typed the portentous question on the keyboard of her recently acquired computer. It was a second-hand machine. Knowing little about them, she had placed herself in the hands of a very pleasant and capable young salesman at the Dean Cross Computer Exchange. She had been somewhat reticent about her actual needs, but the salesman was very patient and understanding. Certainly, it could perform the simple task of word-processing, but it was actually a quite advanced model, with a most intriguing supply of software already installed. He had put the computer through its paces; she had been impressed; she had bought it, considering the price to be quite reasonable—which it was.

Two days later, the computer, its monitor, an impressive array of manuals and a brand-new ink-jet printer had been delivered to her Edwardian terraced house in Laburnum Avenue. She had unpacked it with excitement and set it up in the parlour, with the expert assistance of her twelve-year-old great-nephew. She had mastered elementary word-processing in a matter of six or seven evenings, and was now embarking upon her great experiment, opening the Internet.

Heavy drapes covered the window, and the room was illuminated only by a glimmer of light from the coal fire burning in the cast-iron grate. It was not easy to see the keys on the board in front of her; the monitor screen was hidden under the redundant cover from an unoccupied parrot-cage. By lifting the hem she could view the contents of the screen, but when she let it fall, the harsh phosphorescent glow vanished from sight. Supplanted, at least for the time being, the Ouija board reposed in the large cupboard by the chimney breast, along with the crystal ball, the tarot cards and all the other paraphernalia of Madge Butterworth's lucrative hobby. This evening, she somehow knew, was perfect for contacting "The Other Side". After checking that the message on the screen was correct, she repeated it aloud.

"*Is anybody there*?" she asked in a curious singsong voice.

Then she composed herself, fingers hovering above the keys, eyes closed and her senses alert. Most people in this situation would feel embarrassed, if not downright foolish, sitting in the darkened room waiting for the Spirit World to activate her swollen white fingers, but Madge Butterworth, fortified with a glass of medicinal gin, felt no such qualms. Her belief in the spirit world was sincere and unshakeable, having experienced first-hand some truly remarkable manifestations that could have emanated only from the unseen realm of the departed.

Her forte had been "automatic writing". The spirits, for some incomprehensible reason, strongly preferred the old-fashioned slate to the pen or graphite pencil, and would have no truck at all with ball-pens. Sadly the arthritis, which had seized her ancient knuckles, had robbed her of the ability to manipulate the thin slate pencil, and she had never been happy with the operation of the ouija board. That curious device was terribly slow, and prone to fraudulent manipulation by members of the circle who activated the erratic movements of the little wheeled platform.

She had once received a most disgusting and distressing communication whilst two youths had been resting their fingers on the device. She felt she would never live down the embarrassment, since the vicar's niece had also been present at the séance. The computer appeared to be the answer to a prayer.

Outwardly calm, but with pounding heart, the old lady waited for the first faint tingle that might indicate that the souls of the departed had taken command of her wax-white fingers...

She waited in vain; nothing stirred her fingers, and the screen remained obstinately blank. She lowered her hands to the table and pondered. Wendy, her seven-year-old spirit guide was the daughter of a cordwainer (whatever that was) who had died in 1849. She would have no more understanding of the purpose of a computer than a cat might have of astro-navigation. The whole thing had been a waste of money!

It was at this moment that Wendy's voice spoke from beyond the vale of tears "Did you summon me, Madge?"

"There you are! Thank goodness. Will you find Chief leaping Elk and tell him that I need his help. I've bought a computer—c-o-m-p-u-t-e-r—like the old Ouija board he's used to, but a lot faster, and it will "do a printout" if I understood that nice young man in the shop. Now, go and find the chief, that's a good girl...

• • • • • •

"No, computer—c-o-m-p-u-t-e-r. It's a sort of machine," Wendy explained.

"Ah, machine! Machine—like the great iron horses which gallop heap fast along metal rails across the lands of my fore-fathers, belching steam and smoke onto the tepees of our tribe." Chief Leaping Elk nodded sagely, brushing a limp headdress feather from his eye.

"Well," said Wendy, "It's a different sort of machine, I've been told. No Smoke. No wheels; and it doesn't move anywhere."

"Then of what use is it?" demanded the chief, shaking his noble head and dislodging the loose feather.

"How should I know? I'm only a little girl and I've been dead for years and years. Computer—that's all I was told. I should ask Albert about it if I were you. He's the brains around here." With that, she vaulted onto a passing single-seat cumulus cloud and waved goodbye to the Chief, who, in keeping with his morose disposition, invariably travelled by nimbus if he had any distance to go.

Chief Leaping Elk found Albert Einstein precisely where he expected him to be—sipping hot chocolate in the little cafe by the fountain. He was furtively trying to reassemble a dismantled Rubik's cube. He took a sip from the steaming mug. "Ach! More sugar I am needing," he spluttered, stirring it vigorously with a small slide-rule.

"How!" said the chief.

"Rather should we ask 'why?'" replied Albert. "Pull up a chair, and this proposition we discuss."

Chief Leaping Elk had had too much experience of Einstein's convoluted thought-processes to become embroiled in a philosophical debate. "What is a computer— c-o-m-p-u-t-e-r," he asked sharply.

"What, indeed! Another of the eternal enigmas, my feathered friend. What, which, when, where, whence, who (or do I mean whom?) and, above all, why; curious, is it not, that so high a proportion of the great philosophical questions with the same letter should begin. Let me see... English alphabet of twenty-six letters consists..." He licked his slide-rule clean, turned over a menu card and produced a pencil from his pocket. "Now, assuming..."

With a deep sigh, the chief stalked silently away. If Einstein really were so clever, why could he never answer a simple question?

The chief nodded to the group of figures at the next table as he passed; Napoleon, Abe Lincoln, Beethoven, Madam Curie, Sir Francis Drake, Florence Nightingale—the usual bunch. They were enjoying a pleasant discussion (all were fluent English-speakers, of course) but he knew instinctively that, despite their awesome average I.Q., it would be idle to imagine that any of them could help with his problem.

At length he reached a close-mown field on which many white-clad figures were playing a game that he knew was called cricket. He shook his head mournfully. "Paleface ritual; heap cruel," he observed to no-one in particular, as he watched W.G. Grace hurling a big round pebble at a man armed only with a stick. "Crowd die of boredom." He walked on, dejected.

Ten minutes later he met a schoolboy, complete with blazer and cap. He looked a little bewildered, and the chief correctly identified him as a relative newcomer to the land of spirits.

"How!"

"How do you do?"

"How do you do what?"

"What!"

The chief gritted his teeth. He demanded, "Do you know what a computer — c-o-m-p-u-t-e-r — is?

"I should do, I'm a master hacker!"

"Pleased to meet you, Master Hacker. What is your first name?"

"Jimmy."

"So be it, Jimmy. Now, what's a computer?"

Jimmy Thompson explained, and a smile came over the face of Chief Leaping Elk.

· · · · · ·

So it was that the Chief first made spiritual contact with Madam Blavansky's computer, or rather, with her fingers, causing them to dance over the keys like two small, demented bunches of bananas: "garbage in; garbage out," they say...

When the Chief's message, an extremely long one, ended, Madge bade him farewell and looked up her instructions on how to operate the printer. Moments later, three sheets emerged one by one from the slot. She picked them up, barely able to contain her excitement. She turned on the light and removed the cover from the screen, to discover a single word that appeared in large letters filling the screen: "How," it said. She lit a cheroot, and with trembling fingers, took the sheets over to the comfortable armchair.

She turned over the first of the sheets. Neatly printed, perfectly justified to both margins, was a stream of complete gibberish—numbers letters and symbols jumbled together in utter confusion. The other sheets were just the same. Bitterly disappointed, she rose from the chair, switched off the computer and hobbled from the room.

• • • • • •

A couple of days later her great-nephew called on her after school.

"How's the computer," he asked eagerly.

"Don't talk to me about computers!" she said with venom. "Here, I'll show you what it's done." She opened a drawer and flourished the sheets at him. He took them from her and stared at the incomprehensible mass of letters. Then, with a look of pity at his antique relative, he strode into the parlour and switched on the computer. Removing the parrot-cover from the monitor, he called up the last entry, which was Chief Leaping Elk's "Message"; she had not had the heart to touch the machine since. She watched the lad as his fingers moved swiftly over the keyboard.

He beamed at her, somewhat smugly. "Don't you see, Aunt Madge, you didn't save it like I showed you, but I've managed to get it back. Now, if I just press this button, we'll see what the message really was."

He pressed the key triumphantly, and on the screen appeared words, real words, correctly spelled, spaced and punctuated. It was a story, which began:

MANUSCRIPT FOUND ON A COMPUTER

"IS ANYBODY THERE?"

"Madam Blavansky," known to confidants as Madge Butterworth, ...

Mirror Image

Five minutes—a mere three hundred seconds: that was the margin by which Trevor Marsh missed the arrival of the letter.

The postman parked his red mail van by the gate of 23 Belvedere Drive, and walked up the crumbling asphalt drive to the shabby 1920's house. Its paintwork was flaking, its windows dull. The right hand door of the garage was permanently open, hanging at a slight angle from the perpendicular. Trevor Marsh, it must be said, was letting down the neighbourhood more than a little. The postman dropped the bulky letter through the flap in the front door then went on his way, whistling tunelessly. By that time Trevor was nosing his Astra into the traffic at the junction with Carter Lane. Had he delayed his departure by just those three hundred seconds, he would have met the postman and taken the letter to work with him, and events might have taken a different turn. As it was, the letter lay face-down on the doormat, awaiting his return....

That evening he unlocked the front door, and jolted its frame expertly with his shoulder. It juddered open and he entered. He picked up the envelope, and on turning it over, was distinctly surprised to recognise the spidery writing of his Uncle George.

George Marsh was a cantankerous recluse, who spent most of his life in his wheelchair or in bed, being paralysed from the waist down. It was almost two years since Trevor had visited the old man, and had been made to feel most unwelcome. Although Trevor was his last close relative, Uncle George had had little to say to him, and most of his remarks had been vitriolic. He reveled in his isolation, regarding even the infrequent calls of the postman as an invasion of the privacy he valued above all else. His meagre requirements were delivered by various rounds-men. They left his supplies in the glazed porch, and collected his next order from the little shelf behind the door. Very occasionally a letter, ready stamped, would be left there, with a curt request that it be posted for him. He paid for his goods by cheques also left for collection, so there was no need ever to speak to the delivery people who were his sole tenuous link with the outside world.

His house, a small, detached Victorian villa, was much too large for his needs. It stood in an isolated hollow almost half a mile from his nearest neighbour. Over ten years ago the Highways Department had leveled a sharp dip in the road outside his house. This had necessitated the construction of five concrete steps from the new pavement level to his garden path, and the payment to him of a modest sum in compensation for the inconvenience caused. In truth, he viewed the development with pleasure, the steps, and the newly built wall serving to isolate him still further from the unwelcome world beyond.

Despite his grave disability, George Marsh seemed to have a constitution of iron. If, during the last decade, he had ever suffered anything more than a minor ailment, no one had been aware of it. No doctor or Health Visitor had darkened his doorstep for more than a brief unsolicited consultation through his letter-box. He refused even to consider having a telephone installed. Trevor had twice offered to pay for this essential lifeline, but had met with nothing but abuse. Since his paralysis, the old man's world had been confined to the ground floor of the house, where he had his extensive library and his collection of ancient gramophone records. He had never bought a television set, although he did possess a small radio. Occasionally he was aware of the faint scurrying of mice, or possibly rats, in the abandoned rooms over his head, but thoughts of their depredations did not concern him. In his own strange fashion, he was a happy man.

With these thoughts in his mind, Trevor weighed the letter in his hand. It was heavy, obviously many pages long, and it appeared to contain a small, hard object. Trevor's curiosity was aroused. If the old boy were ill, a brief note would surely have sufficed; if he were not, then there was, presumably, no great urgency. Although intrigued, he put the matter aside, physically as well as metaphorically, as he was in a desperate rush. He was already behind schedule, having already been delayed at work, and by unusually heavy traffic on the way home.

His talents as an amateur artist had been commandeered to assist with set-design and scenery painting for the local amateur dramatic society's production of "The Cherry Orchard". Now, the unexpected illness of the delectable Iris of "The Beauty Box" had suddenly demanded his continued service to the production; he had been asked to stand in for her as makeup artist. So it was that Iris's large box of grease-paints, brushes, cotton wool and tissues were locked in the boot

of his car. He barely had time to snatch a quick meal before leaving
for the little theatre in which the Lambourne Players were due to give
their penultimate performance. Uncle George's letter would have to
wait until his return. Indeed, it could wait until the next day, which
was Saturday. After all, two years is a long time to wait for a letter,
and a few hours could make little difference. If anything untoward had
happened, he could drive to his uncle's house in less than an hour. He
placed the letter against the clock on the mantle-piece, and dismissed
the matter temporarily from his mind.

Trevor did not awaken until two thirty on the following afternoon.
He stared at the clock in disbelief. Never did he sleep so late! However,
he had had a series of very late nights at the theatre, and was desperately
short of sleep, a vivid nightmare having disturbed his nights several
times during the last fortnight. Each time he had awoken to the sound
of his own screaming, yet he had been unable to recall more than a
fleeting glimpse of the images that had tormented him. He had striven
to recapture and exorcise the demons of the night, but they remained
hidden in the shadowy recesses of his mind. He reached for his trousers
almost tumbling out of bed in the process. After rummaging through
the pockets, he realised that the cigarettes were on the kitchen table.

Some minutes later, whilst brewing a mug of strong coffee, he
glanced at the clock and, with a jolt, noticed the still unopened letter.
His uncle had used flimsy old-fashioned "bank" paper, and the close-
typed letter ran to several pages. It had evidently been produced in
great haste, errors had not been corrected and the typing was clumsy
and uneven. Fastened to the back of the last sheet with transparent
tape, was a front-door key. This he removed before settling down at
the table to read. There was a hand-written cover note. It was difficult
to read, but Trevor persevered, and eventually he was able to decipher
it all.

Dear Trevor,

*Something terrible is happening in this house,
and I am powerless to do anything save implore
you to assist me--to rescue me from this, --this
abomination, which even as I write, is somewhere
in the room, plotting my destruction. I can feel
its clammy presence around me, waiting its*

opportunity... My life, or my sanity, perhaps, is in danger, and I can call upon no-one but you to save me. The village people think I am mad; not without reason, for my recent behaviour must appear insane to those who have not witnessed the torments which are visited upon me.

That you may better understand the nature of my terrible situation, I enclose some notes I have compiled during the last few horrific days. I intended no one to see them. In setting down this record I hoped to exorcise some demon within my own mind, but I can no longer take refuge in the thought that I am suffering from some temporary delusion which will evaporate like mist before the sun. I now know that this 'dream creature' is a tangible entity, an intelligence which seeks to engulf me.

I beseech you to read the notes with care, and in their entirety, with the knowledge that they are not merely the ramblings of an unhinged mind. The creature I describe is invading my wasted body and my mind for some unthinkable, godless purpose of its own.

Come to me, Trevor. In the name of all that is clean and holy, do not fail me. Help me overcome this foul creature of darkness. Save me from-- I know not what!

Your uncle,

George Marsh

As he read, Trevor felt the hairs on the nape of his neck rising. His heart pounded in his throat as he picked up the typed sheets. To anyone else, his uncle's letter would suggest nothing more than the ravings of an eccentric old man driven insane by his self-imposed solitude and his own imagination, but to Trevor they carried the ring of authenticity. From his own recent sequence of nightmares, there remained only the awareness of some malevolent presence, which had reduced him to whimpering terror in the darkness. There seemed to be some inexplicable connection between his own nightly torments and the letter before him. He forced himself to follow his uncle's wishes, hoping against hope that the typewritten notes would contain some clue regarding the nature of his own elusive nightmare.

• • • • • •

October 11th

I can no longer convince myself that the strange sensation which recurs each evening as I prepare for bed is simply a foolish fancy, no longer persuade myself that the thing I saw reflected in the mirror was but a weird hallucination or trick of the light. A few minutes ago I tried the experiment which tells me that my fears are justified--that I am the helpless victim of some malignant force; OR--that I am mentally deranged.

The fear that I may in some way be unbalanced forces me to observe strict secrecy (not difficult, in my particular circumstances); but the even greater terror that I may NOT be so afflicted compels me to set down some record of this frightful ordeal.

It is now twelve years since the accident which confines me to my wheelchair, and despite the initial reassurances of the hospital specialists and my own doctor, it soon became clear that I would never walk again. Functionally my legs are sound, although now badly wasted through lack of use. It was expected that I would be back on my feet within a few weeks, but this was not to be. Despite several regimes of treatment, many of them excruciatingly painful, and after countless examinations and endless sessions with psychiatrists, I resigned myself - not without a sense of relief - to life as a cripple. I adapted

well, adjusting my existance to the changed
circumstances with surprising ease. My doctor I
dismissed; now I am almost tempted to write and ask
his advice, but in view of recent developments I
dare not!

· · · · · ·

    At this point a double line was ruled firmly across the sheet; the
remainder was left blank. George Marsh apparently thought that he
had begun his account in the wrong order, possibly missing some clue
that had been present in his early experiences. At all events, the next
sheet began with some of his earliest recollections that might have had
some bearing on his present situation: —

· · · · · ·

As a child I was hypersensitive, and for this
reason I was taken at an early age from the school
where I was remorselessly tormented by my peers.
My parents were always remote, always too high in
the hierarchy of my circumscribed little world to
appear as mere human beings to me. My tutor was
kindly and understanding, and though he did much to
reassure me, replacing my father in my affections,
he was too old to become a real companion to a
highly-strung boy such as me. My childhood, then,
was essentially lonely. This may possibly serve
to explain the origin of my craving for solitude
following the accident.

I was, I suppose, about ten years old when my
recurrent nightmare first occurred. Even now, in the
cold light of day, it still terrifies me to think
of it, to confront its inexplicable loathsomeness.
When I have set it down on paper, perhaps I shall
be able, for the first time, to laugh at its
absurdity - to put it into its true perspective. It
is all too horribly clear in my mind, but no mere
description can convey the irrational terror of the

experience itself.

It started abruptly. I was alone in a large, dimly-lit room. The walls were of roughly-hewn stone, and the small windows set so high that through them I could see only the leaden sky of dusk. In spite of the austere design of the room, its furnishings were lavish. Two large, faded tapestries depicting medieval hunting scenes hung either side of a huge open hearth in which a dying fire flickered and flared spasmodically, providing the only illumination. My eyes caught the glint of polished steel, and as my eyes became more accustomed to the semi-darkness, I could distinguish a suit of armour by the wall. It stood stiffly to attention, but with one arm extended as if pointing to some distant object lurking in the darkness at the opposite end of the chamber. There I could detect nothing but a vague dark shape.

As I began to pick out more of the silhouette, a feeling of unreasoning terror steadily built up within me until I felt I must scream out. I clenched my teeth and forced myself to take a faltering step towards the shadow, my body tensed, leaning forward, hands extended slightly before me. The object proved to be nothing more than a grotesque, over-embellished Victorian china display cabinet, but for some reason, it seemed to be imbued with some indefinable aura of evil.

As I moved away from the fire, there was an answering creak from the shadows at the cabinet end of the room. I froze, rooted to the spot, but the sound from out of the darkness continued, a soft, grating noise, as if some heavy object were being pushed over the broad polished floorboards. Horrified and inarticulate, I slowly retreated. Try as I would, I could not divert my eyes from the cabinet, which seemed to be advancing slowly

but purposefully towards me. It slid with a dull
rasping sound, which reverberated inside me until I
felt rather than heard the movement. It built up,
grinding and pulsing within my body, pounding at my
ribs, choking my throat like hands, until I felt I
could neither shout nor breathe. Still the cabinet
moved towards me, its right-hand side always a
little in advance of the left. My slow-motion
retreat was halted as I felt the cold, rough touch
of the wall against my back. I flattened myself
against it, helpless, and filled with a terror that
seemed to emanate from the case before me, and
built in intensity with its approach.

Closer, closer, it edged its way inexorably towards
me until it was almost within reaching distance.
Just as I felt I must collapse, or be engulfed by
its presence, it stopped, and for the first time, I
looked inside, terrified by the thought of what I
might find there, yet powerless to prevent myself
from doing so.

The cabinet contained nothing but mirrors. Dozens
of them, of different sizes and shapes, but every
one of them inclined at the precise angle required
to reflect my face. In spite of the near darkness,
I was able to see the images as clearly as if it
were broad daylight. No two mirrors reflected the
same face, yet every face was indisputably my own,
but in some way deformed or mutilated. One had a
broken nose, another the bloated face of a drowned
man, whilst a third was lean, with staring eyes and
bloodless lips. Some were children, others middle-
aged or old, but all were recognisable as distorted
images of my own face.

My eyes flitted from one to another, dreading, yet
somehow knowing what must happen next. In the very
centre stood a mirror which was slightly larger
than the rest. Until this moment, my eyes had

evaded this image, but now they were irresistibly
drawn towards it. It reflected my face just as it
must have appeared at that precise moment, the
face of a small boy, ashen white, with protruding
eyes, a picture of abject terror. I could no
longer bear to look upon any of the other deformed
horrors leering at me from the cabinet, and I
stood petrified, staring at my image in the central
mirror.

Suddenly it shattered into a heap of jagged angles,
to reveal behind it the most hideous vision of all
-- a head so loathsome as to be barely human. The
frightful face was towards me, its cadaverous eyes
fixed upon my own, with a look of intense hatred.
Then, it screamed! I could never describe the
agony of that scream which echoed and reverberated
throughout the immensity of the great baronial
hall. The scream and its echoes coalesced,
augmenting each other in a rising crescendo which
obliterated everything -- room, cabinet, mirrors
and all, casting over my mind a blanket which
obliterated all thought, leaving only consciousness
of that hideous sound and of my own terror. Then,
for an instant - I wanted to BE that terrible face,
and to utter the same tormented scream. My lips
parted and in unison, my own shrill voice blended
with the echoes...

I was awake; screaming wildly, limbs thrashing,
as I crouched by the side of the bed. Despite
Mother's assurances, her reasoning, her eventual
remonstrations, I could not, dared not sleep again
that night. I kept the light on, longing for
daybreak. As dawn approached, I gradually subsided
into a gentle, restoring sleep...

· · · · · ·

As he read, beads of sweat broke out on Trevor's brow and his hands quivered. He gripped the thin paper, unable to divert his attention, even for an instant, from his uncle's letter.

• • • • • •

The dream did not recur until I was some years older, when I was perhaps fourteen or fifteen. Everything was precisely as before. The same gigantic room, the same monstrous cabinet sliding obliquely towards me, displaying those revolting images and that ghastly head behind the broken mirror; and finally that petrifying scream. For four years I was tormented by that nightmare. I must have experienced the agony at least a score of times. After that, it never came again -- until two weeks ago. As of old, I awoke by the side of my bed, screaming uncontrollably. But now, crippled as I am, I found my useless legs twisted together with my helpless writhing. I fought alone in the darkness, struggling on the narrow bridge between the terrors of my dream world and the dark drab world of reality. Gradually I dragged myself to safety, to sanity, wearied and aged by the combat. Had I weakened, lost my resolve, I knew I would never have survived.

At last my hand found the switch of my bedside lamp and flooded the room with light. My little chamber was instantly transformed into a haven, a tiny, bright capsule surrounded by an infinity of blackness and evil which pressed inwards all around me; held at bay by the minute, white-hot filament within its fragile envelope of glass. A lion may be held in check with a bit of stick, but should the bluff fail for an instant, should the lion realise his power...

But the light did not waver. At length I heaved myself back onto the bed, where I lay exhausted and helpless, praying ceaselessly for the light of day.

It was the following evening whilst shaving,
that another terrifying incident occurred. For
convenience I use an electric razor. I had just
fitted the plug into the socket when I happened to
catch a glimpse of myself in the glass. I almost
screamed aloud, for in that instant I saw the face
-- the head -- of my nightmare! I took a deep
breath and looked again; the loathsome image had
vanished -- or had, perhaps, existed only in my
fevered imagination... I forced myself back to
reality. I touched my face. The skin felt firm;
the cheeks were not hollow, as they had appeared
in my vision. The eyes, it is true, were a little
bloodshot, but surely this was only to be expected
after the torment I had endured through the night?
I started to shave, but it was impossible to
eradicate the memory of this incident from my mind.

That night the horror stalked me again, a heavy
sleeping-draught having done nothing to prevent
it. When I managed to put my light on after what
had seemed an eternity of groping for the switch,
and eventually regained something of my composure,
I felt that there had been some subtle difference
in the dream on this occasion. In spite of my
loathing, I had to find out if it were so. For
the first time, I consciously recapitulated the
nightmare...

Realisation came as a sickening shock; the dream
had indeed changed in one small detail. The thing
was AWARE! Somehow, it was reacting, responding,
to my moves, tracking me down like an animal. For
one of the mirrors the one on the extreme right
of the top shelf, was now a shaving mirror. It
was identical to the one I had used a few hours
earlier. How can I describe the agony of my vigil
until the dawn? The night seemed endless, and my
lamp more fragile than ever. At last it was over;
the first feeble rays of dawn crept into my room. I

slept.

LATER
When I thought of shaving again, my panic returned.
I could not bear to look into the mirror in case my
tormentor returned to haunt me again. What would it
matter whether I shaved or did not? I live alone;
there was no one to notice that I had failed to
shave that day. I would not shave.

No sooner had I resolved my problem than a new fear
arose: the faces of my dream were all my own, even
that terrible head. Each of them represented what
I might become as the result of accident, disease
or extreme age. Only one of them wore a beard; this
one was -- the FINAL image! I had to shave. If I
refused, I would be accepting defeat-- I would be
passively, if not deliberately, aping that hideous
face, as I had so often counterfeited its scream.

I took my razor from the drawer and plugged it into
the socket. Calmly and resolutely I reached for the
mirror and placed it on the desk in front of me as
I sat in the wheelchair. I adjusted the glass so
that I could see my face clearly and in full light.
It was perfectly normal, not a trace of the thing
I feared. I placed the head of the razor to my jaw
and pressed the switch. Nothing happened. I pushed
the plug more firmly into the socket and tried
again. Still no response. Frantically I jiggled the
switch, but to no effect. I glanced at the mirror
and froze as I caught a glimpse of the face. It was
a cruel, triumphant smile. Then, in an instant, it
was gone. My own face, ashen and unshaven, stared
back at me.

I dismantled the razor, but could find no trace of
a fault. I tried other sockets but to no avail.
I took it to pieces again and again; spent hours
trying desperately to get it to work. By this time

it was late evening. I had eaten nothing but a few
biscuits all day, so I forced myself to prepare a
meal, which I ate with no enjoyment. I sat at the
table for a considerable time afterwards, trying
to delay the call of sleep, with its attendant
horrors. Eventually I was forced to capitulate. I
heaved myself, fully clothed, onto the bed, leaving
on both the bedside lamp and the ceiling light. I
am not by nature a religious man, but I prayed with
all my might that I might be granted a reprieve
from the nightmare for just one night.

Next morning I woke to find daylight streaming onto
my bed and a gentle breeze stirring the branches
of the bushes outside my window. I felt a new
man. Gone were the fears of the last few nights.
My prayer had been answered; I could truly live
again. I busied myself with tasks about the house,
making my meals and putting my books and papers in
order on the shelves. I had been neglecting things
recently, but I was now well again and would put
things right once more. I cleaned and dusted, and
to prove how great was my new-found confidence, I
polished every mirror without a single qualm. I
looked intently into my shaving mirror. The stubble
on my chin was unsightly, but my eyes were not
nearly so bloodshot. The razor still refused to
work, however, so I decided I would leave a note
for the rounds-man, asking for a safety razor. I
also left my electric razor, requesting that he
take it to the electrical shop to see if it could
be repaired.

The day wore on without foreboding. Whilst I was
preparing for bed, I wondered what I should do
about the light. To leave it on would be to admit
that a vestige of my fear remained, whilst to turn
it off would be foolhardy. I considered the matter
for some time, deciding eventually to leave it on.
I fell asleep almost immediately, reveling in such

a feeling of security and well-being as I had not
experienced in many days.

I awoke screaming and struggling on the floor
in total darkness after having experienced the
nightmare once again. I thrashed my arms about
in search of my bedside light. Locating the flex,
I felt along it until I reached the switch, and
flooded the room with light. I knew I had intended
leaving it on, indeed I remembered distinctly
having opened my eyes briefly before nodding off,
just to reassure myself. Had I unconsciously
switched it off in my sleep? I stared at the switch.
It's the type you press once to turn off, and press
again to put it back on. To my horror, I realised
that I had had to press it twice whilst feeling
about in the darkness; the switch must have been on
all the time. It must be defective. Faulty, like
the razor... In desperation I stared at the wall
switch. It was in the 'on' position, yet the bulb
was unlit.

That day (yesterday, in fact) was another
uneventful one. When I had recovered sufficiently
to drag myself into the wheelchair, I tried the
wall switch. It now works perfectly, but when
I first tested it I had to flick it up then down
again before it functioned. This is an old house,
and it should probably be rewired. But I am an
old man. The cost does not bother me, I am not
without means, but I would hate the noise, mess
and disturbance which would be caused if I were to
have the work carried out. No, the old wiring is
getting a bit unreliable, but no doubt it will see
me out. I've been much better during the afternoon,
and realise that I will have to learn to master
this experience myself. Confront it. Overcome it.
It's not good placing my faith in a bit of new
electrical wiring, my salvation, like my problems,
must come from within.

The rounds-man took my note. I was watching him
discretely from behind the curtain as he came up
the path with my milk, a small loaf and a few
other odds and ends I had requested. My needs are
few. He's a good, reliable sort of chap, although
it is years since I actually spoke to him. I
wonder if he is aware that I watch his every move
whenever he calls...? Probably not. Anyway, he very
thoughtfully scribbled a note for me, and put it
through the letterbox. He said he would get the new
safety razor I had requested and return my electric
one as soon as possible. He is a thoughtful man, as
I have said, and I may even open the door and thank
him personally when he calls. I'm not quite sure
whether I am yet quite ready to meet anyone again.
Certainly, with three days' growth of stubble and
my sunken, bloodshot eyes I will perhaps refrain
for the moment. But who knows, in a week or so, I
may pluck up courage. By then I will have shaved.
My stubble is growing surprisingly quickly. It's
already beginning to look like a beard. A BEARD! My
God, that's the last thing I want!

4.30 p.m.
After I wrote the above I pulled myself together. I
had a thorough wash and a meal then I did something
I had not ventured to do for perhaps two years -
maybe even longer. I wheeled myself to the front
door and, unfastened the lock. Then with some
difficulty, I edged my way through the porch and
opened the outer door. I propelled myself up the
ramp, and found myself in the open air. The garden,
left entirely to its own devices for many years,
was unbelievably overgrown. I must hire a man to
do something about it. It was a beautiful day, and
I wheeled myself right up to the steps which give
access from the road. Someday, perhaps, I may even
consider...

Anyway, a few minutes in the open was sufficient.

I pivoted with some difficulty on the narrow path, and returned to the house. My house: my prison! But prison it will be no longer. I will open my door and speak to the rounds-man when he calls. This dreadful experience may be the making of me after all!

October 15th

My euphoria has gone, and with it all my hope! The dream occurred again last night. As is my custom, I had left both lights burning, but they were out when my ordeal took place. When I switched them twice, they came on. Electricity is beyond me. I really must get the place re-wired.

The most ominous thing is that the dream has progressed further. All the mirrors but for the central one, now resemble my shaving mirror, and all of them reflect my face just as it now appears -- old, worn, unshaven and repulsive.

I hear the gate-latch. Yes, the rounds-man approaches!

10:45 a.m.
I have done it! I had ensured that I did not lose my courage when the time came. I had left the inner door slightly ajar, and placed a note under the knocker, which is stiff with years of disuse. It read "Rounds-man - door open. Please come in." And in he came! It was as simple as that! I called to him from the study and he found his way to me. Thank heavens I had made the house respectable to receive my first guest for years. I'm afraid I did not make a favourable impression upon him, however. I have not been accustomed to social intercourse for a considerable time, and my appearance must be far from reassuring.

Mr. Rawlings, for that is the man's name, is tall, with sandy hair, a host of freckles and over-large teeth. He's an amenable enough fellow, but I am sure he looks upon me as something of an oddity. Perhaps he thinks me a simpleton - in my dotage. I've been a recluse for a long time; conversation does not come naturally to me. But I am not in any way mentally abnormal. By no means.

Mr. Rawlings brought back my razor. There was no charge. The man at the electrical shop had tested it, and it was working perfectly. Mr. Rawlings plugged it in and demonstrated that all was in order. In the circumstances, he had ignored my request for a safety razor. He did not want to take a penny for his pains, but I insisted upon his taking a generous tip.

He seemed to know a little about electricity himself, so taking my courage in both hands, I led him to the dining room, which for so many years has served as my bedroom. There I showed him the faulty switches. Without mentioning the dream, of course, I told him of their erratic behaviour. He asserted quite bluntly, that what I was saying was impossible. He tried both of them repeatedly, and they operated perfectly. "Could there be a problem with the wiring?" I asked.

He shook his head. "Impossible to say without a voltmeter, but it looks okay to me. It would cost quite a bit to rewire the place, but a mate of mine would give you a fair quote, if you are interested. If I were you, I really wouldn't bother."

Rawlings refused a drink, although I had produced a fair bottle of Port, and my best crystal glasses were on a salver on the sideboard. He seems an honest man. I will give the matter of re-wiring some thought.

11:40 a.m.

I am hoist with my own petard! After Mr. Rawlings
left, I tried the razor again; it simply will not
work, and I am still without a safety razor. I
tried every socket I can reach, but there's not a
flicker of life from it. My portable radio works
perfectly well from the same sockets, so the razor
must be at fault. After our long discussion about
it I dare not approach Rawlings again on the
subject. I'm certain he already considers me 'odd'.
If only I dared to take him into my confidence and
explain why the razor is so vital to me. But I dare
not; if I were to tell him about my dream, he would
think me totally insane! No, it is unthinkable. I
must tell no one of my ordeal until I have quite
recovered.

October 16th

My persecution continues. Last night was more
horrific than ever. The strain is manifested in
my mirror, which reveals a repulsive face, which
now closely resembles the face: the face of my
nightmare! I dared not sleep. I kept both lights
on, and lit candles. I also had a pocket torch,
which I tested carefully. I sat writing at my desk
with a large flask of black coffee. I am attempting
to change my habits - trying to sleep during the
day, and remaining alert at night. Several times
I felt myself nodding and managed to jolt myself
back to wakefulness. I played my radio loudly, and
from time to time I wheeled myself up and down the
room, and when the candles started to burn low, I
replaced them with new ones. I'm running a bit low
on them - I must remember to put a note out for
Rawlings.

Time dragged unbelievably. My eyes ached
abominably. I had to rest them, just for a moment.

I drifted into sleep.
This time the dream was radically different. I was
in the same dismal room as of old, but gone was
the glass-fronted cabinet that had so often struck
terror into my soul. In its place, a long low shape
rested on the floor, dimly visible in the sinister
gloom of the chamber. As my eyes grew accustomed to
the dim light, the shape began to assume a definite
form, and a wave of loathing shook my body. The
ominous shape was a coffin. As the cabinet had done,
it began to slither slowly over the shiny floor
towards me.

Unable to flee, I retreated, my eyes fixed on the
moving form, until I felt the cold stone against my
back. There I slumped to my knees, transfixed, as
the form continued its relentless approach. I could
make neither sound nor movement, but waited like a
small creature mesmerised by a snake. How far must
the shadow progress before it was upon me? Several
yards - and at that snail-like pace, the journey
would take some minutes. Five minutes, perhaps? No,
- less! How far now? The floor was highly polished
and around the hearth, it reflected the tongues of
flame from the open fire. To reach me, the coffin
must pass over this illuminated area, this sole
remaining patch of hope. How far, oh Lord, how far
now?
The shape passed over the glowing patch as if it
were glass. My faint ray of hope was extinguished.
At last, inches from me, it stopped, and my eyes
were drawn to look directly at it, expecting to
see some unspeakable horror within… The coffin was
empty!

A cold sweat broke out all over my body and all
life seemed to have been drained out of me, leaving
me a mere shell. I rose to my feet, shaking and
trembling, still staring into the black void before
me. That hideous scream rang out - proceeding from

the empty coffin. I pitched forward into the gaping
chasm. The blackness engulfed me: the blackness
of my own room, where I found myself struggling
and screaming on the cold floor. The lights were
out, and would not come on at all. The candles
were entirely burned away. Only the pocket torch
would now work, and for the remaining hours before
daybreak I crouched in my wheelchair, pointing
the pathetic little beam of light all around the
room, waiting for some movement in the darkness.
Some unseen entity, an amorphous presence, seemed
to reach out from the void, only to slide away,
evading the enquiring cone of blessed light.

October 17th

As I write, I know that I am doomed. My adversary
is a power beyond the comprehension of Man. I
have been tracked down remorselessly, like some
sacrificial animal. It could have destroyed me
whenever it wished, but it has preferred to torment
me like a cat with its prey. The power is within
this house, and it now prepares for my complete
annihilation. I cannot escape. It knows and
rejoices that I am a prisoner, taunts my useless
legs, tampers with lights and razors, and has
jammed fast the door. Soon it will reach towards me
from a darkness of its own making. I no longer have
any vestige of hope…

● ● ● ● ● ●

So ended the frightful document. George Marsh had sealed it into
its envelope, stamped it, then pushed it out through the letterbox, with
a note imploring Mr. Rawlings to post it without delay. Next morning
Rawlings found it on the floor in the porch, shaking his head sadly as
he read the frenetic message. He rapped on the door, but there was
no answer. With a lingering look at the drawn curtains, he turned and
retreated up the path.

Trevor had not read the letter in its entirety. In fact, he read only
the first few pages of the long manuscript before stuffing it into his

pocket and racing to his car. Crashing the gears, he lurched from the drive, spinning the wheel madly as he turned onto the road. He raced along, ignoring the traffic lights, with horn blaring, desperately trying to regain lost time.

He knew his uncle was eccentric, and would have been willing to think that the old man had lapsed into total insanity, but for one harrowing fact—it had been about a fortnight since his own nightmares had commenced. Each time he had awakened from them he had been unable to recall the nature of the terror which had afflicted him—mercifully, it had been banished from his mind. His uncle's account had brought his own horrific visions to the surface. The dreams were identical! How was it possible for two people to share the same nightmare?

He drove like a maniac, finally slamming the elderly car to a halt on the main road by his uncle's gate. Clutching the key from the letter, he wrenched open the gate, almost stumbling down the steps in his headlong rush to reach the door.

George Marsh had been dead for some time before Trevor's arrival.

The key had proved useless, and he was forced to smash a window to gain entrance. His uncle's body sprawled on the floor by his desk, face downwards. His clawed hands were by his head, as if trying to ward off the blow of some unseen attacker. Prepared, as Trevor was, for some terrible revelation, the corpse proved to be even more revolting than he would have thought possible. He turned it over, gasping as he caught sight of the loathsome face. The dead eyes seemed to gaze straight into his own, their expression of sheer hatred and malice piercing his very soul and sapping the strength from his body. The sunken cheeks and matted beard, the long unkempt hair made the contorted face almost unrecognisable as that of his uncle. The skin had a scaly appearance, and seemed ready to part in flakes from the shrunken flesh.

This, Trevor knew, was not the face of his uncle; it was the creature which had haunted him in his dreams: had haunted them both. It was dead, but its very existence was a mockery of his own. The apparition had somehow ousted Uncle George from his own cold body for its own purpose. The thing before him was the physical embodiment of the creature of their dreams, and it had to be destroyed.

With considerable difficulty, he opened the front door from the inside and dashed to the car, from which he took a small bundle. It contained the makeup equipment he had placed there the previous evening; an evening that seemed so remote and trivial beside the dreadful task which lay before him.

He discovered the electric razor plugged into the wall socket beside the desk. He switched it on, and with a shudder, commenced his work. At first he was so nauseated that he dared not look at the face itself, focusing his eyes on the rotating heads of the razor, telling himself that he was merely preparing another actor for the play. It took a surprisingly long time. As he finished his task he noticed that dusk was approaching. The dense foliage of the overgrown shrubs in the garden and the dull windows further reduced the pale light filtering into the room.

He strode over to the wall, only to discover that the light-switch was already on. Perhaps the bulb had failed—he would take one from another room. He pushed the switch up, then down again. Instantly the room was flooded with light. Uttering a gasp of relief, he returned to the body. Out of curiosity he tried the razor again. He fiddled with the switch repeatedly, but it no longer worked.

His next task was to close those staring eyes, which seemed to follow his every move as he proceeded. Getting the lids to close was neither easy nor pleasant...

The face had now lost some of its terrors, but the loose scaly skin must be covered over. He applied a thick layer of foundation cream, working it into the creases and furrows with his fingers until there was a clean, reasonably smooth surface upon which to work. Next he must give the face some colour and character. He found it difficult to remember just what his uncle had looked like. It was several years since he had seen the old man, and there was no photograph of him to hand. However, he knew that there was a strong family resemblance between them; the fact had been remarked upon several times in the past. If he could make the face resemble his own, that would be sufficient.

He picked up a shaving mirror that stood conveniently on the table nearby, placed it on the floor, and angled it to examine his own features. Yes, there was a resemblance even now; the same domed brow, the same nose and slightly protruding ears. His uncle's hair, although long and tangled, was the same colour and despite the difference in their ages, receded to the same extent. His own face, then, would make an excellent model.

One big difference, however, was the sunken cheeks of the corpse. They must be padded out. Feeling into his pockets he came across the letter. Smiling grimly, he crumpled up some of the thin sheets and prising open the jaw and lips, forced the pads into the grinning mouth. He had great difficulty closing the lips again afterwards, but eventually he succeeded then commenced the operation of converting the bland face into a replica of his own. Glancing from time to time at his reflection he worked on, applying paste and make-up with a skill he had never thought possible before. Soon the image in the mirror and the face of the body were identical save for the hair.

He rummaged in Iris's bag and took out the scissors. It seemed an impossible task, then, remembering that his uncle used to cut his own hair with an old hand operated clipper, he opened the drawer of the dressing table and found it immediately. Trevor had never used one of these devices before, and wondered at his uncle's skill in managing to cut his own hair with it. Removing just a little at a time, he began to get the feel of it, and after a few minutes, he was able to control them quite well. After much trial and error, he eventually achieved a reasonable approximation of his own style. He swept up the bulk of the shorn hair with the hearth-brush and dropped it into the waste paper basket.

At last his odious task was finished and he started to gather his things together. He felt a real sense of accomplishment in having obliterated all trace of that ghastly phantom which had destroyed his uncle, and had haunted them both in their sleep. For what had seemed an eternity, Trevor had been crouching uncomfortably by his uncle's side, and now that he came to rise, found that the circulation in his legs had been severely restricted. He struggled to get to his feet, but the pain of the blood rushing back into his arteries was too great; with a yelp he sank back to his knees. He would wait a little, then...then... what would he do? First he must report the death. The awful truth struck him—what would the police make of his actions? He could not tell them the whole story—they would think him mad...*MAD*!

A fresh wave of horror shook his body. Perhaps he *was* mad; he must have been mad ever to have done such a thing. Again he tried to rise but his legs would not obey. Struggle as he might, his legs were useless and he was in agony. Suddenly he had become a cripple—a cripple like his uncle: *mad*, like his uncle. He gazed at the face of the corpse again. The lips had begun to gape again, giving the features a wry, mirthless smile. Did he himself have those faint sinister laughter-lines around the mouth, those slight creases at the corners of the eyes, or had he unwittingly added these nuances of expression to the corpse, making it more life-like? Suddenly this became a vital issue. Did he, in fact, have that sardonic smile himself? He had to know!

Frantically he searched for the mirror. He soon spotted it, out of reach on the easy chair where he had tossed it on completing his work. He dragged himself across the worn carpet, still unable to rise because of the excruciating pain in his legs. He clutched it in his hand, and held it up to his face.

It was then that all hope fled. The face that peered triumphantly back at him was that of the dream creature.

He caught only a fleeting glimpse of the leering image before the lights went out of their own accord....

Untitled Manuscript

They removed the bandages from my eyes almost half an hour ago. My God! — the light!

When I asked, they told me it is Sunday, 14th March, 2027. I didn't ask the time and there is no clock in the room. No watch on my bedside locker. No clothes in the little melamine wardrobe. I looked out of the window and judging by the long shadows that were creeping across the lawn from the trees by the high brick wall, I guessed it must be about 5:00 p.m. The window doesn't open—at least not the bottom section, so I can't lean out to discover how big this place is. Obviously, it's a hospital, but it's very quiet, and there is very little in the way of medical paraphernalia in the room. A private room, it seems. I suppose I could just open the door and look along the corridor. But I don't want to do that. Not yet. This tiny world, with its hint of a bigger world outside, is enough for the present.

When they took the bandages off there were two of them, a nurse and a junior house doctor with a stethoscope round his neck and bags under his eyes. I was barely conscious, probably sedated, but I asked them for a pen and paper. At first they refused. "I'm afraid we must run a few routine tests, Mr. Farrington" the doctor began—but I got agitated.

"Farrington?" I demanded.

"Yes", he said, glancing at the chart hanging from the end of my bed, "Farrington."

That's not my name! It's... it's..." I stopped, for the very good reason that I couldn't remember my real name; but it's not Farrington. It couldn't be. It just doesn't "feel" right. Anyway, everything suddenly went blurred and I realised that tears were running from my eyes. That was when I lost my temper.

That doctor is amazingly strong for his size. Or perhaps I'm a lot weaker than I thought. He pinned me down to the bed just by gripping my upper arms and pushing me gently down. He whispered something to the nurse and a few seconds later I felt a jab of pain in my thigh. Soon I was calmer, and asked to be alone. Well, they agreed. Before they left I asked again about this pen and paper. The nurse came back with a few sheets of A4 and a cheap ball-pen. I'm not sure I want them now—there's not really very much to say.

Apparently I've been in some sort of accident. A car, they said. Concussion. And some trouble with my eyes. Not much wrong with them now! I can see some daffodils under the trees and they must be fifty or sixty yards away. And I can see the tip of my pen as it wriggles over the paper leaving a trail of words. Badly written, I must say. Perhaps I've lost a bit of co-ordination—surely this isn't my writing. But of course it is. I'm writing it, so it's my writing—but I'm sure I didn't write like this before. Farrington. Farrington. That's definitely not right. I'm sure it's not. They've got it wrong. Got the papers mixed up or something. Amnesia, they said, as if that explained everything. Or anything!

Damn funny business. I can remember all sorts of things. Remember? Well, come to think of it that's not really the case. I know lots of things, but I actually remember little or nothing. Let's see, now —"If you pricked me, would I not bleed?" That's Shakespeare—or a paraphrase at least—so I do have some sort of memory. I know a joke about amnesia. Scene: an American Police station. A seedy looking little guy in a battered top hat and torn clothes is pacing up and down and one cop is saying to the other "No, he still doesn't remember who he is - but he's certain it's someone pretty damned important..."

I used to think that was a good joke. Now I'm the little guy, I'm not so sure.

Monday, 15th March, 9.35 a.m.

They've given me back my watch. Pretty expensive-looking, despite its cracked glass. That happened in the accident, no doubt. They've also returned my glasses. My glasses, indeed! I don't need glasses. They fit perfectly, but they are just slightly tinted low-power reading glasses and I don't need them. They aren't mine, anyway. Belong to this Farrington chap. Note written inside the lid of the case: "Edward Farrington, 117 Chelstoke Road, Pinner." Never been to Pinner in my life!

(Thought: — how do I know I've never been there? Perhaps I have —the fact that I don't remember doesn't mean a thing. Come to that, how do I know that I'm not this Edward Farrington who wears tinted reading glasses?)

Well, yesterday they did their tests. Pretty routine stuff—nothing to get excited about. Seem to think I'm doing pretty well. Not too worried about the amnesia. They say my memory could return any time - hours, a few days, possibly a few weeks, but it should come back all right, maybe in dribs and drabs but possibly in a great surge... Then they dropped the bombshell! My wife is coming to see me this afternoon! My wife! I don't have a wife. I don't, I don't, I *don't*!

I *could* be this Farrington, I suppose; but I'm not married. Definitely not. Anyway, they'll have to admit their mistake when she doesn't recognise me. Come to think of it, she's in for a pretty nasty shock - expecting to find her beloved Edward here in this private ward, and she'll walk in to find me sitting here wearing his watch and tinted glasses. Actually, the glasses do seem to help a bit when I'm writing. Anyway, why hasn't she been to see me every day—that's what wives do, isn't it?

The nurse (different nurse, this time) told me why not. My "wife" (this woman) was with me when we crashed, and she was knocked about a bit herself. Apart from this amnesia business and a painful lump on the side of my head I don't seem to have a scratch. Perhaps I should be visiting her, but they wouldn't hear of it. "She's fine, now" the nurse told me, but you are to stay as quiet as possible for another day or two. Then we'll see."

"I feel fine, whoever I am" I protested. "By the way, can you tell me what happened—it's time someone did. What did I hit?"

"I'm afraid I don't know much about it, but I understand it was a head-on crash with another car. The other driver was dead on arrival. He'd been drinking..."

Just then her bleeper started and she dashed out of the room like a bat out of hell.

Well, about this wife business. This could explain it. She must be the wife of the other driver. If so she's in for one hell of a shock. Doesn't even know he's dead! In about an hour's time she's going to enter this room, an expression of concern and sympathy on her face and a bag of fruit in her hand, to discover a total stranger who killed her husband! This really is awful. I'm going to ring for the nurse and tell her what's happened, then she can warn the poor woman—take her away and give her a sedative or whatever.

I pressed the button and she came running. Not quite the same breakneck dash as you see on TV, she's a rather elderly, buxom woman, but she managed a fair turn of speed, all things considered. I told her that she must intercept this *Mrs. Farrington* and break it to her gently. She got me back into bed, looking very concerned, and said she would sort it out. What a relief!

It's very hot in here and I'm feeling a bit drowsy.

3.20 p.m.

So I *am* Farrington! David Farrington, proprietor of Farrington's bookshop, Pinner.

My wife Elizabeth—apparently I call her Liz—arrived at 10.30 and was shown in by that nurse after all. She was carrying a bag of fruit as I expected, but there my scenario ended and reality took over. I was in bed and woke as the door opened. Liz dropped the bag of fruit on my locker, leaned over the bed and flung her arms around me. She engulfed me, her long silky black hair cascading about my head as she pressed her full moist lips to mine, whilst her perfume—an expensive one, I suspect—seeped like tendrils into my very being. Soon her warm tears were trickling onto my face.

Farrington, I thought, you lucky buggar! You have taste in women, I'll grant you that! The plaster on her forehead in no way detracted from her beauty. Indeed, its rough texture served merely to emphasise the unblemished softness of her skin. And those eyes! Huge dark irises, almost as black as her hair...

She stayed with me for over an hour. The nurse made a discrete withdrawal as we clinched, and did not re-appear until half an hour after Liz had left. We had talked, between bouts of cuddling, of our home, of friends and the garden, in which she apparently takes a great deal of interest. It all went over my head, of course. No bells rang. No flashes of illumination lightened the darkness within my skull. Desperately I blunder about in the void of my mind searching for Liz, but I recall nothing from the past—from before the time she re-entered my life like a blazing comet. She's tall and slender. As for getting to know her again—well, I can hardly wait! And I won't have to wait long—if all goes well I should be home tomorrow.

Two policemen came to visit me about an hour ago, wanting a statement, but it was a waste of time, I could tell them nothing. In fact, they told me a lot more than Liz or the nurse had done. Putting all the data together, it seems that at about 6.30 five nights ago (how times flies when you're amnesic!) Liz and I set off to attend a local amateur dramatic production of "Charlie Girl". It was raining and almost dark. Liz was driving. About half a mile from the theatre this lunatic came round the corner, going far too fast, on the wrong side of the road. Liz braked hard, but the other car crashed head-on into us.

Some locals dragged us from the wreckage—we were all three unconscious—and laid us out like a row of dead fishes on the verge. Just as well they did, because a fire started and both cars more-or-less blew up in a ball of flame. By the time the Police, an ambulance and a fire engine arrived Liz was coming round, but this maniac and I were still out cold.

They piled all three of us into the ambulance, but the other chap died before we reached the hospital. He was called Andrew Stevens, and his car was some sort of continental job with a left-hand drive. For some reason I can't quite put my finger on, that bothers me—the left-hand drive business, that is. Anyway, his skid marks, along with the level of alcohol in his blood completely exonerates Liz. His fault entirely. There should be no difficulty about claiming on his insurance. That's a thought—I wonder what sort of money Liz and I have? How much profit does a bookshop make? Does Liz work? If so, as what? Do we have any other source of income? One thing's for sure, this watch, Liz and her clothes, the car we had (it was a pretty new battery-powered Montgomery tourer). These things don't come cheap—we're certainly not on the breadline.

Naturally I'm a bit worried about the bookshop. Running it, I mean. Will I be able to cope if my memory doesn't come back properly? I expect it will just come to me naturally—like riding a bike; I suppose. I don't ever remember actually riding one, but if I walked out of here right now and found a bike by the entrance, I know I could just get onto it and pedal away without even thinking about it. Probably the same with the bookshop—just set the auto-pilot and everything will be all right. I wonder if I have an assistant of any sort? I suppose I will find out soon enough.

Something still niggles me about this left-hand drive business. Stevens' car was a left-hander—I wonder if our Montgomery was, too? It's just that I somehow "feel" myself driving from the left-hand seat. Curious. I know I'm getting very close to a real memory at this point. With a bit of luck it could be the start of actual breakthrough.

Tuesday, 16th March, 2.30 p.m.

We got home by taxi, mid-morning. Home turns out to be a very "des res" on the outskirts of town. It's a three-bedroom bungalow in a third-of-an-acre plot, and Liz is rightfully proud of her garden—she tends it exclusively herself. Probably as well, somehow I don't see myself as a weed-puller.

On the way here we passed the scene of the accident. No debris lying about, of course, but two fair-sized trees have been pruned hard back (no doubt their charred branches were a potential hazard) and a section of pavement and a wall are blackened. The sight had no effect on me whatsoever. No flash of memory, no feelings of panic or disaster. Nothing.

Liz has gone out to visit a sick cousin who lives two or three miles away. Pleading tiredness, I declined to accompany her. She was very understanding. The plaster's off her head, by the way. Looks a bit painful, but it shouldn't leave much of a scar, thank goodness. Lacking a car, she wheeled a bicycle from the garage and rode off down the sloping drive. In a way, I'm glad she decided to go—really I want to be alone to get my bearings and to think. These notes help to keep things in perspective and they will be interesting to look back on when I'm back to normal. Somehow I feel secretive about them; even a little ashamed, for some reason. I certainly don't want Liz to read them. Not yet, anyway. So I hide them and only write them up when I'm alone.

We seem to be pretty solvent, judging by the quality of the furnishings. Liz does have a job—her own beauty salon in town, which has been kept ticking over by her two assistants since the accident, but she intends going in tomorrow and Saturday which are the busiest days.

We have a cat, by the way—a big pewter-coloured Persian, which for some inscrutable reason, is called Jennings. Well, I like cats and Liz told me that Jennings dotes on me, but I certainly didn't get that impression when he pushed his way through the cat-flap into the kitchen. He saw me immediately and bounced towards me as if he were leaping through a field of long grass. Calling his name, I crouched down, extending my hand towards him. Suddenly, two paces from me, he stopped. His back arched, his fur stood on end and he silently bared his teeth. Then, in a flash, he was gone - fleeing into the sitting room like a thing possessed. It took quarter of an hour to gain his confidence and that was only after he heard the sound of me opening his tin of meat. Even now he clearly regards me with grave suspicion. This worries me a lot. I have a great respect for the instincts of the domestic cat. He knows something is "wrong" about me. And so do I. I'm still not convinced that I am Edward Farrington, bookseller of Pinner.

Jennings seems certain I'm not.

Wednesday, 17th March, 10.20 a.m.

God! What a mess I am in! Last night was a complete and utter disaster in every respect. I don't know who the hell I am, but I'm trapped in the body of a total stranger!

Liz phoned me as soon as she arrived at her cousin's to ask if everything was all right. I reassured her and she said she'd be home at about five o'clock. I promised to have a pot of tea ready to brew the instant she arrived. I spent some time slouched in an armchair reading newspapers to catch up on recent events. There seemed to be no appreciable gap in my knowledge. World events, political intrigues and tittle-tattle all fell into place in my mind, much as if I had just returned from a brief holiday abroad. But my personal life remained an obstinate blank.

Later I opened the drop-front of a rather elegant Georgian secretaire in the smallest of the bedrooms, which we apparently use as a sort of study cum office. Inside I found some of our business accounts, which didn't tell me much, except that Liz seems to be the real bread-winner here.

There was also a big album containing scores of photographs of kith and kin all lined up in orderly rows like butterflies pinned out in an entomologist's cabinet. Neatly printed underneath, in Liz's minute writing are the "field notes" and identifications—Aunt Sarah and Uncle George at Scarborough, July, 1947; Cousin Arthur with his new motorbike, 1953; unknown relation of Edward's—great-aunt Esmie? —and so on. Looking more closely I realised they were divided into two series "His and Hers", and there were two rather incomplete family trees. All total strangers to me.

I put everything back and closed the desk. Nothing to do with me; even though I had seen my own face looking back from the pages of the album. Mine and Liz's. Liz is a very beautiful woman. No wonder her salon is thriving. Her makeup is minimal but extremely effective, emphasising those huge eyes. Her clothes are unbelievably svelte— even the denim trousers she wore when cycling looked as if they had been made to measure. Perhaps they had. As she rode off, I noticed that her long glossy hair was scraped back and tied in a pony-tail. I looked in her wardrobe. Nothing but the best—exclusive brand-names, all of them. Most of her lingerie, like her makeup, is minimal; mere scraps of gossamer and lace.

Anyway, by the time she got back I had gathered up various odds and ends of information about us both and tried, successfully, I think, to give the impression that my memory was beginning to return. Liz bathed and changed before we had dinner at about seven - she had popped a super-market frozen lasagne into the microwave. Pretty awful. Says she's not much of a cook, and I can well believe it. I can do better than that with no effort at all. Whilst the crockery was being blitzed in the dishwasher we settled down to watch a film on television. I sat in a big fat armchair. Liz perched on one of its wide arms, but after a couple of minutes she swung her long bare legs across me and slid onto my lap. Her skirt rode up to the thigh and her silk blouse gaped as she placed her slender arms around my neck and pulled my face to hers.

Then we were rolling on the thick-pile carpet, clutching desperately at each other, kissing and gasping. Sloughing off her blouse, she took my hands and placed them over her small firm breasts. "We'll soon see how serious this amnesia is. If you've forgotten anything important I'll soon remind you!" With that she sprang nimbly to her feet and undulated in the direction of the bedroom, stepping neatly out of her skirt without breaking her stride.

She was like an animal! Her long red nails gouged deep scratches on my back as she churned against me uttering guttural moans and occasional squeals of exultation. Her demands were insatiable and at times unbelievably crude. It appalled me to hear the words issuing from those perfect rosebud lips. It went on and on until I was almost sobbing for mercy, but at last she was done with me. "You are out of practice, my love," she said. "I shall expect better of you tomorrow." With that she kissed me lightly on the brow and turned out the light.

No doubt most men would be overjoyed suddenly to discover that they had unknowingly married a beautiful, wealthy, lusty young nymphomaniac, but I was shattered, mentally and physically by the savagery of her onslaught. I am still sore and I don't think I can face another such night. Perhaps my best defence will be attack. Last night she raped me; tonight I intend to take the initiative.

Thursday, 18th March, 11.00 p.m.

Edward Farrington is dead. Long live Andrew Stevens!

I've half suspected the truth for some time, but the reality is more incredible than the make-believe world I have inhabited since the crash. I am now convinced that I am Andrew Stevens, somehow trapped in the body of a bookseller who is married to a nymphomaniac. When I look into my shaving mirror it is the haunted thirty-nine year old face of Farrington that peers back at me. But Farrington's spirit—his Ka, his Id, his *élan vitale*, call it what you will—was cremated inside my mangled body two days ago!

She—Farrington's wife—returned from work by taxi at six-thirty, looking radiant in a black suit with a pencil-skirt and a pure white silk cravat at her throat. Dinner was almost ready. I had prepared a spaghetti bolognaise and it was superb although I say it myself. Liz was very impressed. "Unsuspected talents! It's the first time I've ever known you cook anything which is actually edible. This really is excellent. The wine, too."

I had found an acceptable if undistinguished bottle of wine in one of the kitchen units, and there was ice cream with fresh fruit to follow. "I wonder what other talents you've been hiding," she said with a pointed leer. Her words sent a jolt through me. I am a good cook - I just know it, but why wasn't she aware of it? A small thing, in itself, but too many anomalies were mounting up.

"Tell me," I asked, "Was our car a left-hand drive? Silly, I know, but I just don't remember."

She looked at me curiously. "Of course not—why do you ask?"

I managed to shrug it off, but inwardly I was becoming steadily more perturbed. My total lack of memory I could accept, but things like my sudden ability to cook, the strange response of the cat and my feeling about driving a car from the left made me feel very ill at ease.

"Do you know anything about Stevens?" I asked casually.

"Who?"

"Stevens—you know, the maniac who crashed us."

"No, not really. Oh! That reminds me, I forgot to show you. There was a bit in the local rag on Tuesday. I cut it out and put it in the letter-rack."

She retrieved it and handed it to me. It didn't say very much. A brief mention of me and quite a paragraph about Liz—"Former Beauty Queen in Horror Crash." Stevens was dismissed very briefly. Tough, that, since he was the one who actually died. Perhaps there will be an obituary next week. Aged twenty-three. Unmarried. Worked at the Claremont Hotel. That was it; but it was sufficient to set me wondering whether he was a chef, or a kitchen assistant at any rate. There was just one stock photograph—of Liz as Beauty Queen, naturally.

Whilst Liz loaded the dishwasher, I retired to the sitting room and turned on the television mid-way through a natural history film. As it was ending, Liz made her coquettish entry, wearing a flimsy lemon negligee under a fur-trimmed night gown and carrying a glass of wine in either hand. She placed them on the coffee table, then perched on the arm of my chair. This time I was prepared...

Perhaps I went too far, but it served the bitch right. She slept in the spare room afterwards.

Friday, 19th March, 10.30 a.m.

I woke screaming, in the small hours. Liz did not come to comfort me. It is possible that she slept through it, of course. Being a gentleman, of sorts, I give her the benefit of the doubt.

In my dream I had been driving my elderly Peugeot rather too fast. I was angry and in a hurry. I'd had a drink or two, but nothing I couldn't handle. Just as I got to that nasty tree-lined curve, a big dog loped into the road. Nothing wrong with my reflexes! Instantly I wrenched the wheel and missed the confounded animal by inches. As I began to straighten out, this flashy silver Montgomery tourer came hurtling round the corner and we crashed head-on. They had the benefit of airbags and a sound chassis, but my safety belt did little to protect me. The steering wheel smashed into my ribs and my head snapped forward. I lost consciousness.

Then I was floating, without pain, suspended above a scene of chaos where three men were dragging bodies from the crumpled cars. A sort of misty umbilical cord tethered me to my shattered body, which was being lowered onto the grass verge. Slowly the cord started to contract, drawing me downwards, but I wrenched and struggled, determined not to be hauled back into that doomed shell. The cord parted, and like a swimmer I struck powerfully towards the other body.

I began to enter it, my feet, ankles and calves progressively dissolving as I moved vertically downwards. Just as my waist began to meld into the flesh I noticed that another umbilicus was manifesting itself and looking up, I saw the form of Farrington above me, desperately trying to reach and eject me from his body. I was younger and fitter than he, but he attacked like a madman, raining kicks and blows as I sank slowly into his body.

In desperation, I grabbed his umbilicus and took it into my teeth. It was like biting into a garden hose-pipe, but I wrenched and tore at it like an animal. I saw the look of horror on his face as it finally parted and he realised that I had gained possession of his mortal body. With a lunge he made for mine, knowing nothing of the shattered ribs that had penetrated its lungs. Farrington was beginning to enter the prostrate shell feet first as I had done, when my head slowly sank into the warm flesh of his body. He must have realised that my body was about to breathe its last, and glowered at me in impotent fury.

At that point I woke, screaming, from the nightmare—knowing at last that I am that shadowy figure, Andrew Stevens, hotel worker, living parasitically within the body of one Edward Farrington.

4.30 p.m.

I am writing this in the lobby of the Claremont Hotel. My memory, now that I am searching for the right identity, is fast returning. It's rather like watching a photographic print developing in its dish of chemicals. For a long time the paper is blank; then vague ghostly shapes begin to appear. At first the shapes are amorphous, ambiguous, but with increasing speed they resolve themselves into coherent images and the complete picture suddenly reveals itself.

There is one major difference, however—the photographer watches with some interest and anticipation, yet he can be fairly dispassionate about the process, since he knows in advance what will be revealed. But when the emerging image represents a forgotten aspect of one's own innermost being, the operation is charged with awesome significance. Especially if, as in my case, one is appalled by the revelation. Watching the pupal case split and expecting some exotic butterfly to appear, I have witnessed the release of a loathsome scorpion—myself.

Yes, I am Andrew Stevens, Sous-Chef here at the Claremont. No one recognises me of course—my borrowed shell is a perfect disguise. At the same time it precludes me from resuming my own life, such as it was. I can neither return to my former life, nor continue my pseudo-existence as Farrington, whom I murdered as surely as if I had butchered him with one of my razor-sharp carving knives.

In a moment I am going to walk boldly into the kitchen I know so well and pick up one of the knives that I know will be clipped onto the board over the work-top... God forgive me for what I have already done, and for that which I am about to do! I cannot forgive myself, nor can I continue to manipulate Farrington's body as if it were a puppet. Liz will mourn "his" passing, no doubt, despite recent troubles. She will forgive him, retrospectively.

And she will look well in black, her peach-blossom cheeks glowing beneath her mourning veil...

Take Two

Things got under way as midnight commenced at the Greenwich Meridian.

"Final scene—TAKE ONE! " said the Lord.

The Aurora Borealis sprang into life with such unprecedented vigour that it could be seen from the equator, whilst ten thousand multi-coloured comets wheeled, blazing brightly, through the firmament. For good measure, a dozen super-novae, triggered in readiness untold aeons before, became visible from Earth, where 1763 volcanoes erupted simultaneously in a spectacular orgy of sound and colour.

Oceans boiled, and the air was rent asunder with lightening which coruscated above the wondering world. The clouds glowed, incandescent with every known shade of red orange and yellow, with here and there, a subtle hint of purple, colours reflected from the concatenation below. Miraculously, using the word in its most literal sense, no one was killed, which could have led to all sorts of unnecessary administrative complications.

From deep space, the celestial P.A. system blared forth with the definitive rendition of Haydn's "Depiction of Chaos", followed by "Ole Blue Eyes" proclaiming "I did it myyyy way!"

Neville Porter of West Hartlepool woke briefly from a deep dream of pizzas, and muttered something about "Bloody neighbours", and "Sodding barbecues". Hoping it would rain, he pulled the covers over his head and went back to sleep. He was one of very few exceptions; elsewhere people were on the streets, on the beaches, in the hills: they would never slumber. Portents and manifestations portended and manifested like tadpoles in a duck-pond.

"Hey up!" they exclaimed in Lancashire.

"Gosh, I say, steady on," they remarked in the Home Counties.

"It's a braw and moonlit nicht!" Glaswegians proclaimed when the Earth's nearest neighbour began to pulse rapidly and a gigantic neon sign flashed the single word "GOODNIGHT" in every known language, extant and extinct. For some inscrutable reason, the Swahili version appeared upside down, to the consternation of those who could read it. "Cor, stone the crows!" expostulated one of the few Swahili-fluent Cockneys.

"CUT!" commanded the Lord, as He picked up His celestial calendar. He tapped it against His other hand. "Blessed thing's on the blink again," he said bleakly. "Drop penultimate scene, take one, and wrap. Lose the props. We'll try a new take tomorrow."

With a sense of relief the Seraphic Host relaxed, then began redirecting the comets, turning off the moon-sign and the P.A.. system before painstakingly feeding red-hot lava back into its conical containers. Cherubs busied themselves eradicating all trace and memory of the fiasco.

"TAKE TWO!" commanded the Lord.

This time everything went smoothly, and He held up His thumbs with satisfaction, and the final scene commenced.

A billion graves yawned. From the depths of the oceans, from the dry dust of the deserts, from beneath ice, tundra and savannah, from tilled fields and tarmacked used car lots, the departed—well, departed.

The lion lay down with the lamb, to the consternation of the lioness, who had other plans that day.

"Now hold it right there, already," exclaimed the Lord. "Just cut that out right now. We've quite enough problems as it is, without any more chimeras. I've still not decided what to do with all those mermaids and centaurs. The basilisks, the cockatrices and all that bunch have gone off to... the other place. We did a deal. My life! What a deal we did."

One of the unwitting beneficiaries of "the deal" was the same Neville Porter who had more-or-less slept through Take One. In his case it had proved unnecessary to erase his memory of the previous night's embarrassing anti-climax, but the usual after-effects of several pints of Newcastle Brown consumed before the first tentative fingers of the Northern Lights had appeared, were thankfully absent.

Alone, he observed the landscape around him. It appeared much like the English Lake District, as it might have been depicted by Walt Disney on one of his *really good* days. It had been created expressly for Porter; his specific fantasy of Paradise

Into Porter's private dream-world strode a true "gentleman of the road", complete with flowing beard and twinkling eyes. "Well met, my good friend Neville Porter. Pray allow me to introduce myself — I am

God."

"God!" exclaimed Porter somewhat scornfully, as he looked the newcomer up and down. And who is your tailor? I must be sure to avoid him."

The stranger laughed heartily. "Judge ye not by outward appearances. Were I to appear in the panoply of My normal guise, you would be overwhelmed by its magnificence and overawed by My presence. These rags were selected to put you at your ease, for I wish to have a little chat with you. To welcome you; make a few suggestions about places of interest, things to do, people to meet and so on."

"A bit over the top, isn't it?" Porter persisted, still eyeing the threadbare suit and down at heel brogues. "Or do I mean under..."

"A man of discernment! Well, seeing that you are so fastidious, I might as well change into something a little more comfortable." There was a brilliant flash of light, and the stranger was suddenly clad in a loose-fitting toga of dazzling white.

Porter was impressed, make no mistake! No TV commercial could begin to compete with that, he thought with awe. It was worn with casual grace, hanging loosely round His splendid form, which appeared to have grown several inches during the transformation.

"Lovely bit of material; just feel the quality..." He proffered the hem of the toga. It certainly was very fine cloth. "Omphalie spun the thread for it. Clever girl, that. She'll go far."

"But... but, Omphalie didn't do any of the spinning!"

"No?"

"No, it was Hercules, apparently. In drag. Omphalie made him do it while she swanned around wearing a lion-skin or something."

"You're quite sure about that?"

"That's what Miss Briggs, my teacher in primary school taught us."

"Just goes to show, doesn't it? Still, lovely bit of schmutter, eh?"

I say, you're not... well, I mean..."

"What? Spit it out, my lovely boy!"

"Well, of the Judaic persuasion?"

The Lord laughed heartily. "A Jew! Well, a lot of people seem to get that impression, but it's purely subjective, you know. Comes from your own predilections; that must be how you've always thought of Me. I am all things to all men. Lots of Buddhists tend to see Me as a sort of re-incarnated leopard, a praying mantis, or an eagle—something of that sort. All perfectly valid, of course..."

"What are you really, then?"

"I am that I am…"

And with that Porter had to be content. He gazed at the poignantly beautiful country around him. "Excuse me, but where is everyone? Surely I can't be the only successful candidate in the book of the Recording Angel? I mean, why am I getting all your attention? After all, I'm nothing special…"

"Well, to use a golfing expression, you only just made the cut, but you made it, my boy, you made it! Now, about the others—you'll meet them in due course, but you see 'Today', although the term is now without meaning, of course, is what we call Receiving Day. I decided to have this preliminary chat with everyone, all at the same time, of course. That's one advantage of being Omnipresent.

"It's said you are also Omniscient— is that true?"

"Let me just think about that…"

"If you need to think about it, you aren't, surely?"

"Don't be so hasty. At the moment I'm a bit preoccupied. This has all been a bit of an upheaval, you know."

"All those graves! I understand."

"Not quite what I meant, but let it pass."

"Where are the famous Pearly Gates?" Porter asked, a tinge of disappointment in his voice.

"Well, somehow you managed to come straight in the back way— the trades person's entrance. I knew we should have got those signs fixed. Anyway, you wouldn't have seen the Pearly Gates, even if you'd come the official way.

"No? How's that?"

The Lord shuffled His feet and looked a little uncomfortable. "Well, to be perfectly frank, as I always am, I was never very keen on them. Very pretty and all that, but not really practical. Always getting jammed. It was very embarrassing at times. Well, in the end, we had them put in the waiting room… the 'Reception Area,' I should say."

"Limbo, you mean?"

"Exactly. We decided to develop it as a Heritage Centre, you see. All pastel shades and silver clouds, harp recitals and so on. The Cherubim had the time of their infinities, of course —all in fancy costumes with great big *papier-mâché* heads, handing out iced manna and pots of ambrosia." He chuckled softly. "Gave the new arrivals something to while away the millennia until we decided what we should do with them. Good family entertainment, of course. No smut. Everything free of charge, naturally. Strictly non profit-making, courtesy of the

Management. Talk about ineffability..." He leaned forward and patted Neville on the shoulder. "Next time..." He began, then broke off with a shake of His head.

It was then that Porter made a most curious discovery. As the Lord leaned forward, the toga gaped, and revealed to his startled gaze, was a navel! He had heard the old debate as to whether Adam was, or was not provided with one of these useless features. The consensus seemed to be that if Man were made in the likeness of God, and God, clearly, had no cause for one, then Adam (and presumably Eve) didn't either—although their descendants down through the ages necessarily did. Now, here was an indication that God Himself had been born! Porter's mind reeled.

"I hope you don't mind me asking a personal question, but... why do you have a navel?"

A hearty peel of laughter rang out in the crystal air, echoing from the distant mountains and momentarily distracting a kestrel that was about to swoop on a juicy shrew, which existed only in the bird's imagination. The actual shrew, was stalking a non-corporeal beetle; the beetle in turn was...

"Navel, Schnavel! This was a bite from a dinosaur. You see, I had this reptile phase at one time. I created all sorts of them, and saw that they were good. Big ones, little ones, some of them with horns and tusks and frilly bits all over. Colourful, too. Quite enjoyed myself for aeons. Anyway, one day I went down there to have a closer look. And did they adore me? Did they bow down and touch their forelocks with their mighty claws? Did they Hell! This great brute of a Brontosaurus upped and bit me. That's gratitude for you."

"But surely the Brontosaurus was a great friendly, half-witted herbivore; I have seen 'Jurassic Park' you know..."

"Ah! The Mark One, yes, I grant you. But the Mark Two was an entirely different kettle of lizard altogether. Regular carnivore, with bad breath and personality problems you wouldn't even want to dream about. Seventy cubits from fangs to tail, if it was a span! Anyway, that's what comes of giving dinosaurs free will, I suppose. Well, I soon put a stop to all that malarkey. Wiped them out, apart from a few rather cute crocodiles and some piddling little lizards. Started all over again. Decided to give the mammalian line a go. I did toy with the idea of birds for a time, but mammals seemed the best bet."

"Then, eventually, you created beings in your own likeness and put them in with all the others?"

"Well, in a manner of speaking, yes; you could put it like that. Seemed a good idea at the time."

"And now You've pulled the plug on the whole thing?"

"Ring down the curtain, the farce is over, I decided. Time, gentlemen, please."

"So what are You going to do now?"

"I wish you hadn't asked. *You'll* wish you hadn't asked."

"Well?"

"Start all over again. A few loose ends to tie up here first, of course, then it's 'The Creation' Mark 277,625. There'll be some real changes this time, you'll see. Or rather, you won't."

"CUT!"

Train of Events

My lawyer wants me to try "The Dodge".

That's not what he said, but that's what it amounts to.

Thorburn, that's his name. He's very short—about five foot four. Wears a midnight blue suit. Very sallow face with a mop of short black curly hair. Worst of all, he has this tic. Every so often the right corner of his mouth twitches upwards and he seems to wink at you. His eyes are light brown. All in all, he looks a bit "seedy"—possibly a bit crooked. Not my idea of what a lawyer should look like, at all.

"We meet in unfortunate circumstances, Mr. Bardsley," he began, shaking my hand limply. His hand is soft, cold and clammy. Not a hand I would care to shake again, but I suppose I'll take it willingly enough if the thing works out.

He asked me all sorts of irrelevant questions to begin with. Not a mention of my case for nearly ten minutes. Understood I was a keen gardener; which were my favourite flowers? Did I watch much television? Was there too much violence on the box? What were my favourite toys as a child? I was getting pretty impatient, as you can imagine. Then, straight out of the blue, he came right out with it —

"Did you murder the girl, Mr. Bardsley?" And he stared right into my eyes. I could almost feel his gaze boring into my brain. Then his face seemed to go all misty—and it dissolved! It took a minute for me to realise that I was crying. Great tears ran down my cheeks and my chest heaved as I sobbed.

"No, I never went near her. I didn't even know she was there until I woke from the nightmare."

"Tell me about it."

He sat there in my cell, seeming very much at ease, apart from the fingers of one hand, which drummed silently on the table between us. He rested the elbow of his other arm on the table, fingers lying pensively against his lips. He never interrupted, never commented or prompted, even though I told my story in a disjointed, stumbling fashion. Towards the end he placed both elbows on the table, formed a steeple and rested his chin on the pinnacle. His eyes were staring vacantly into the space over my left shoulder; he didn't appear to be paying any attention. Appearances can be deceptive.

When I had finished there was a long silence. I began to get fidgety. "Well?" I demanded.

The sleeves of his jacket slipped down a little to reveal his weak, hairless wrists. "I'll be frank with you, Mr. Bardsley. I don't think you made up this story. On the other hand, it is clearly untrue..." I attempted to interrupt but he silenced me. "I did not say that I thought you were lying. I am convinced that you genuinely believe what you have just told me. However, the Prosecution will undoubtedly deduce that you are trying The Dodge."

"What dodge?"

"The insanity dodge. Diminished responsibility. Man-slaughter, not murder."

"But, but...it really is the truth!" I slumped in my chair. "It's true—all of it..." I said weakly.

"In that case we have a problem. If you stick to that story you will either be declared insane, or they will decide that that you are indeed guilty of murder, and are trying The Dodge. Are you quite sure that this is the sequence of events you wish to present under oath, in court?"

"There is no other story. It's the truth, I tell you!"

"In that case, I would like you to have a talk with a colleague of mine.."

"A psychiatrist, I suppose?" He nodded. "What if he decides I'm sane?"

He did not answer my question. "You said you were unwell — 'off colour' was the expression you used—before you boarded the train. Now, this is important and I want you to think carefully before you answer—were you taking any form of medication? Any sort of drug? Had you been to your doctor with the complaint?

I shook my head. "I took a couple of aspirins. It was just a cold. No point in going to the doctor with that. Besides, I didn't have time. I had to dash for the train as it was."

"Your account was disjointed. Incoherent, almost. Perhaps it would be as well to get it down on paper, as clearly as you can. Your statement to the police was a shambles. You need to get it all clear in your mind, and writing it down is the best way."

So that's what I'm going do. Whether I tell the truth, or lie like a secondhand car dealer will make little difference: I'm going to end up either in a cell surrounded by crooks, or in some stately home with stately bars at the window and stately felt all over the walls.

Thorburn opened his briefcase and took out a notepad and a couple of ballpoint pens. He left them on the table for me. He's coming back tomorrow (with this psychologist) and I promised I'll have it ready for him, so here goes —

The 15.47 from Manchester to Carlisle was just over a quarter of an hour late when it pulled into Preston. This was "lucky"—if you can call it that—because if it had been on time I would have missed it by several minutes. It was pouring with rain and I'd got soaked to the skin on my way to the station. I was feeling really sick, with a bad cold and a migraine.

I wouldn't have been going to Carlisle but for a phone-call I'd had around three o'clock. My cousin had rung to tell me that his mother (that's my Aunt Joan) was in hospital after a nasty car accident. I'd had a word with the boss, and he's agreed to let me take a couple of days off so I could have a long weekend with Roy's family, and visit her. In fact, he insisted I went immediately. He noticed I was pale and shivery, and asked Carol (a temp who was working in the office, to get me some aspirin before I left. I wish to hell, now, that I didn't have such a considerate boss!

The train was practically empty. My coach was unoccupied apart from a courting couple right at the far end. As soon as the ticket inspector had visited me I lay down, shivering, on the seat.

The next thing I remember was hearing the door slam and this distinguished-looking old man tripping over something on the floor, and almost poking my eye out with the corner of his bag. He was tall and thin, dressed all in black, like an undertaker setting out for work. But he had a round face with mutton-chop whiskers, and sparkling eyes. Believe it or not, he was wearing a top hat and a black cape with a crimson lining. His shirt had a starched front and a butterfly collar—just like something straight out of Dickens. In fact, he spoke like something out of Dickens.

Once he'd got over apologising and dusting himself down with his pale lilac gloves he sat down, heaving his leather bag onto the seat next to him. It was an old-fashioned Gladstone bag, but I never realised that they made them so big! The train had suddenly become quite full, which seemed rather strange. Even stranger, no one sat near to us, and we had the two longer seats facing each other to ourselves.

After a couple of minutes he opened that bag of his and rummaged inside. "You know, young fellah, you look decidedly under the weather, if you don't mind my saying so. I've got a little something here that might buck you up a bit." He produced a palm-sized flat bottle of ruby-red glass with an ornate silver cap. "I never embark upon a journey without my little friend here," he said, unscrewing the cap, which turned out to be a drinking measure about the size of a small egg cup. He filled it to the brim and offered it to me. The old chap seemed so concerned about my appearance that I thanked him and swallowed the cap-full in one go. At first I couldn't taste a thing—brandy or anything else—and for a few seconds nothing happened. Then it hit me! First, my throat felt as if it had been cut, then my throbbing head seemed to swell up like a balloon, whilst someone appeared to have filled my stomach with boiling lead. These dreadful symptoms passed almost as rapidly as they had appeared, and a sense of wellbeing passed over me. A mist came up in front of my eyes – and everything went blank.

I woke up—God knows how much later—feeling much better than I had for the last couple of days. The old guy was leaning over me, looking a bit concerned. Then he smiled and those little blue eyes of his twinkled like sequins. Suddenly, I sat bolt upright, unable to believe my eyes. We were sitting in a rather dimly lit, ancient coach just like you might see in a railway museum—one without a corridor, made up of lots of separate compartments. Somehow, without my having the faintest recollection of it, we had been transferred into a completely different coach. I recollected that there had been a railway museum at Carnforth—"Steamtown" it had been called. It closed many years ago, but this must be from the collection of rolling stock they had once displayed. For some reason, 'they' must have hitched one of the vintage coaches to our train whilst I had been fast asleep, and moved us into it. We were moving quite rapidly, I could see trees flashing past the window. The whole thing was crazy! Surely wooden-built coaches of this age were illegal except on special excursion trips? What's more, I could hear the wheels going "snickety-snack, snickety snack" just as they used to do before the days of continuously welded track. We weren't even on the main line any more! The train must have been diverted at some point. Had there been an accident? This must be an emergency relief train!

My bewilderment about the coach and our precise whereabouts was suddenly overshadowed by the presence of the girl. She was sitting next to the old man, snuggling up against him, opposite to where I was sitting. The generously upholstered seats ran the entire width of the coach. She was wearing a long cream coloured dress with a high collar and a very full skirt. It wasn't a crinoline, exactly, but it sort of billowed out like one of those illustrations in 'Alice in Wonderland'. She had long dark hair, but most of it was hidden under a straw bonnet. She was very small, but her features were not those of a young girl. She had small, full lips, a flawless complexion and the most beautiful grey eyes, through which she stared demurely at her delicate hands clasped on her lap.

Before I could gather my wits and ask what strange events had led to our present situation, and where the girl had appeared from, the old man spoke. "I'm relieved to observe that you are looking much the better for your nap, young man. May I have the honour of presenting my ward, Mr. – Mr....?

"Bardsley," I responded. "Delighted to meet you, Miss...?"

"Hazeltine; but you must call me Sylvia." Suddenly hesitant, she turned to the old man. "He may, may he not, dear uncle?"

"I should be most offended if our charming companion were to address you otherwise, my dear. However, Mr. Bardsley is, I fear, a trifle indisposed, and I feel it my duty to divert him a little as we travel." So saying, he reached into the bag once more. I stole a glance at the delightful Miss Hazeltine – at Sylvia – but she sat perfectly still, staring fixedly at her slender hands.

"You see, my dear fellow, I am by profession an exponent of the art of legerdemain, a prestidigitator, a worker of wonders, a purveyor of miracles! In short, Sir, I am a magician and illusionist. 'Mandovini', at your service!" As he spoke the last words he rose from his seat, flung back his cloak with a flourish and gave a sweeping theatrical bow. Pushing back his sleeves, he unclasped his bag, reached inside and took from it a plain black cube measuring perhaps six inches across. "Observe," he commanded, tapping the cube with a short wand, which appeared from no-where in his hand. The cube sounded like a solid block of wood. He tossed it into the air, imparting a twist that set it spinning about its diagonal axis. He caught its point on the tip of his index finger. There it remained for a moment, still spinning rapidly, until he launched it gently upwards. It rose slowly, defying the law of gravity as it augered its way through the air until it almost touched the roof of the swaying coach. There it remained, revolving steadily. Mandovini pointed his wand at it. There was a blinding flash and the block vanished. From the spot in which it had hovered, six fresh-cut, long-stemmed roses tumbled to the floor. Gaping in astonishment, I gathered up the flowers and proffered them to Sylvia Hazeltine—but she remained as if frozen, still staring at her hands resting on her lap

Too dumbfounded to applaud this spectacular feat, I sat open-mouthed as Mandovini gave a slight bow before turning and taking a great curved sword from his bag. It was at least a foot longer than the bag itself... "Kindly examine this sabre, Mr. Bardsley," he invited, passing it to me hilt first, in the formal manner of a duelling "second" offering the weapons to the protagonists. It was surprisingly heavy. Until then I had no notion of what a substantial weapon a heavy cavalry sword really was. I have a reasonably strong grip, but I found that it required a considerable amount of force to flex the wicked blade. It was honed sharp as a razor, right to the tip of its snub point.

Mandovini took it from me, and holding it in the middle of the blade, sharp edge uppermost, placed the murderous point in the centre of his gleaming white shirtfront. Then, with calm deliberation, he slowly drove the blade into his body. I watched with mounting horror as the blade slid smoothly through his chest. I almost vomited as he turned to reveal the glittering steel as it emerged inch by inch from his back. I've seen the act performed on stage—I even know how it's done—but I'm prepared to testify on oath that Mandovini's sword was no stage prop, and there was no possibility of substitution: it was a genuine sword and it passed clean through his body. He withdrew it and dropped it to the floor. It landed with a clatter. I looked up to Mandovini's immaculate shirtfront, which seemed to glow with a pearl-like lustre. There was a slit immediately above the heart, and sick in the stomach, I waited for the blood to spurt. But nothing happened.

I must have turned a bit green, for the magician sat down, placing his arm around the dainty Sylvia Hazeltine. "I fear Mr. Bardsley was not amused by our little experiment," he said. "Do you think, perhaps, that Monsieur Blanchard might divert him at this juncture?"

The girl's voice rose in terror— "Please, Uncle, I beg of you, not Monsieur Banchard! Why not perform instead your celebrated illusion of 'The Miser's Hoard'? I'm sure Mr. Bardsley could not fail to be entertained by that."

"I think not, my dear. The miser's hoard is an entertaining enough diversion in its way, but I feel M. Blanchard might be offended if he were to be overlooked in favour of a mere pretty effect." Suddenly he started, as if in alarm, and raised an admonitory finger. "Hark! I hear him." Withdrawing his arm from the waist of his ward, he turned to the bag again. I could hear a faint, muffled voice as he reached into its impossible depths to lift out a rosewood box some fifteen inches tall and perhaps ten inches square. It was the sort of box in which a microscope might have been housed.

He placed it on the seat, then took a small golden key from the watch-pocket of his waistcoat. He inserted it into the brass lock plate, but before turning it, he straightened up and turned to face me. "I feel a word of explanation is necessary, Mr. Bardsley. You see, M. Blanchard was a former rival to me in the art of legerdemain. He was gifted—very gifted: of that there was never any doubt. But the man had the temerity to challenge my indisputably greater powers.

"We chanced to meet on a boulevard one fine summer day in Paris. We were both performing to packed houses in rival theatres in that great city. During the confrontation, Blanchard was so ill advised as to offer me an insult in public. I demanded that he withdrew the remark and tender a formal apology, but he refused. Naturally, I had no alternative but to demand satisfaction. The duel was to be held at dawn next day in a small coppice on the outskirts of the city. However, after the heat of the moment had passed, my adversary must have reflected upon my prowess with cold steel..." Mandovini gestured modestly towards the slit in the front of his shirt. "That evening, after his scheduled performance, by way of encore, he performed his celebrated disappearing act, leaving much of his equipment in the hands of the theatre management!" He chuckled maliciously to himself. Then, suddenly serious, he continued "Unfortunately for M. Blanchard, his too-solid flesh reasserted itself: some days later he was arrested for the brutal murder of a young lady in a railway carriage. The young lady in question happened to by my ward, and invaluable assistant on stage. He was tried and subsequently condemned to death, which in that country, as you will know, is effected by means of the guillotine. So it is, that it amuses me to dub the image featured in my 'talking head' experiment—Monsieur Blanchard!" He turned the key in the lock and flung open the door of the little cabinet with a flourish.

"Behold!"

Once again I felt my stomach lurch as I gazed in horror at the severed head resting on a heap of blood-stained straw. The contorted face wore an expression of unspeakable agony and the staring eyes burned like coals. Again, I have seen similar feats performed on stage, but in the confines of that tiny compartment, the box barely a yard from where I sat, what I saw was grotesquely impossible: there was the head, apparently living and suffering in its miniature rosewood dungeon.

When it spoke I covered my face and slid into the furthermost corner of the carriage. "Bardsley!" it shrieked in a strong french accent "It's too late to save me, but save yourself.

Throw yourself from the train – anything – but escape from that madman whilst you still have the chance. I never touched Sylvia Hazeltine. It was he, Mandovini, who slaughtered her, because he suspected I was her lover. He had me executed for the crime. It was he who..."

The voice rose to a scream of terror, and despite myself, I peered between my fingers to witness Mandovini savagely striking the helpless face again and again with the butt of his heavy cane. Then he slammed the door, locked it and returned the key to his pocket. His face was convulsed with rage.

Groping for the handle of the door, I glanced at Sylvia Hazeltine. She was slumped in the furthermost corner, one leg twisted across the other, her head leaning on her breast. As I began to twist the handle of the door a grin appeared on Mandovini's face, and a peal of laughter rang out above the rattle of the wheels and the creaks of the swaying carriage. He fixed me with his eyes, and spoke— "Tell me, Bardsley, do you not admire my little act? Be honest, do I not detect some twinge of unease, a slight pulsing of the veins in your throat, a tightening of the muscles, some shortness in the breath? Is it fear I detect?"

"Keep back," I screamed. "That head, Mandovini... It's real. You are a maniac!"

Suddenly solicitous, Mandovini took a pace back from me. "Do calm yourself, Mr. Bardsley, I implore. You are allowing your imagination to run away with you. Perhaps I do allow my illusion to get a little out of hand on occasion, but I assure you that I am merely an entertainer. That head is one of my 'props'. Allow me to demonstrate." Re-opening the box, he tenderly lifted out the head. "You see, my friend, one of my modest accomplishments is the art of ventriloquism. And I am an actor of some renown. This poor head is no more real than 'my Ward' the charming Miss Hazeltine."

I stared at the pathetic little figure, which remained motionless in her corner. "That's right," he said "Sylvia is merely a puppet. A thing of rag and wax, motivated by my skill, and given substance by the power of your own imagination. Observe." So saying, he picked up the sabre, which still lay on the floor by his feet. With a lunge he swung it savagely against the little figure, which writhed and shuddered under his onslaught. Blows rained down upon it. Suddenly its beautiful head slumped forward and fell to the floor with a distinct thud. As it rolled towards me, a wake of crimson blood spattered over the floor and across the legs of Mandovini, who was laughing insanely. "Illusion, Mr. Barsley—all is illusion," he managed to gasp.

I felt the scream rising in my throat. Then all went black...

The rest you know, Mr. Thorburn. — How they found me cowering in the corner with my legs drawn up like a foetus. The body of the smartly dressed girl lay on the far seat, her blood forming a viscous pool on the upholstery and trailing in little rivulets over the vinyl flooring. Our coach had reverted back to the twentieth century — rather than the Victorian era — more of Mandovini's insane magic. Sylvia's head lay in the passageway, the long dark hair matted with blood, and those dead, grey eyes staring vacantly into mine.

The weapon, I understand, has not been found. They tell me that the police have combed both sides of the track for many miles in search of it—but they are wasting their time. They will never find Mandovini's sabre.

Did Mandovini end his days in a padded cell, I wonder.

So long as he never enters mine—that's all I ask....

Eternity Trap

"**G**'mornin' Squire! Got our paperwork, have we?"

I stared at the demon in astonishment. He was bright red, as one might expect, and stood a little over four and a half feet tall on his black-tipped hooves. Had he straightened his slender goat-like legs he would have appeared considerably taller.

"Paperwork?" I asked.

"Your PXD 38/B!"

I stared at him in bewilderment. "I'm afraid I've never heard of a PX...whatever. Where would I have got it from and what's it for?"

"Got to have a PXD 38/B! Can't just waltz down here and expect to go straight in without some sort of authorisation. Do you have a TR509 exemption certificate then?"

Gradually it dawned on me that this was the Reception Desk of Hell itself! There had been a monumental cock-up somewhere; at this moment should presumably be standing at the Pearly Gates, exchanging pleasantries with St. Peter.

"Oh dear—it's going to be another of those days! Don't tell me—the usual story—*they've sent you to the wrong place...*"

"I've no idea how I got here. In fact, the last thing I remember was this big black car bearing down on me—then this awful screech of brakes and everything went black..."

"You mean to say you didn't have a post mortem interview with the Recording Angel?"

I shook my head. "Nothing. Total blackout. Then here I am apparently talking to some sort of demon in a rather sensuous art nouveau anteroom. I say—you are *real*, aren't you? I mean, I'm not hallucinating, am I?"

He gave a light laugh. "If I told you I was a figment of your own imagination, would you believe me?"

This flummoxed me for a moment. "Well, let's assume you are real, and that somehow I've been transported to the very gates of Hell. It's all some ghastly mistake. Computer error, probably. Perhaps you can tell me how to get back to this 'Recording Angel' setup?"

"I take it you are familiar with 'Orpheus in the Underworld'?"

"What, the Offenbach comic opera?"

"That's the one, squire!" He started "dah-dah-ing" the famous can-can.

"Well, what about it?"

"Do you happen to recall how Orpheus managed to get down to Hades and back?"

"You mean to say there is a lift or escalator of some sort?"

"Not exactly—but you are on the right lines. Trade secret how it works, but I daresay I could get you back to the Recording Angel's place *tout suite*, as they say in Gay Paree. For a small consideration, of course..."

"You mean...you take bribes?"

"You take whatever you can get in this job! But seriously, you know, you should really think about this. I mean—if you get up there and they decide that—on balance, all things considered, taking one thing with another—you don't have the right credentials to come down here, they will send you upstairs—to the 'Other Place'". Different paperwork, of course. PXD 38/B's don't grow on trees, you know..."

"Now we are getting somewhere! Which way to this 'lift' thingy?" I took out my wallet.

"Not so hasty, squire, only joking! I said you need to think about this a bit. Have you ever wondered what it's like up there, or down here, for that matter?"

"Life everlasting up there, eternal agony down here, of course! Brimstone and ashes... No contest." I opened my wallet and took out a wad of notes. He looked at them and chuckled.

"Chuck them away, chuck them away! Currency is a bit de-valued you see. Utterly worthless, as a matter of fact. Remember the bit about the camel and the eye of a needle... No, just throw it away—there's a rubbish bin under the desk there. Dump your useless credit cards in as well. Some of the lads collect obsolete currency and so on—as souvenirs. I'll share these round, don't you worry. Meanwhile let me explain what happens in the afterlife. Now, you were saying about 'Eternal Life', but have you ever stopped to think what that actually means?"

"Surely it doesn't need any explanation. It just means that you live for ever afterwards."

"Exactly—for-*ever*! Not just an extra life-span or two. Sooner or later you'll realise that you can't actually *do* anything. You see, we are talking infinity here. That doesn't mean the odd few million years on top. They say the first couple of billion millennia are the worst. Then the next trillion or so; and all the others—to infinity! Sobering thought, isn't it, squire? I mean, when you see it in perspective... And what do you actually think you will be able to do in the infinity of time? I mean, it takes just so long to become a harp virtuoso. And what about family life? If your wife doesn't make it up there, (and I understand there's a bit of doubt about that) but that 'holier-than-thou' uncle Joe manages to squeeze in—thanks to a death-bed confession—well, things won't look quite so rosy will they? Will you have your nice blue vintage Morgan three-wheeler up there? Somehow I doubt it. Then there's the question of petrol. Not many petrol stations, so I understand. Think about holidays—where will you go? Don't imagine you will be able to jet off to Hawaii with the Joneses. Actually, the Joneses won't be there to go *with*—I know that for a fact... Even Margate will be 'out'. No pets, of course—they don't possess souls... Just face it—'Heaven' is Hell on Earth! Nothing to do, no-where to go; no joy, no sorrow. Endless ennui. Talk about a life sentence—for infinity!"

"Have you actually been there, or is this all just hearsay?"

The demon chortled. I thought only overfed schoolboys chortled, but he did it, no mistake. "Touché, squire! I ain't never been there. Got more sense, I have. Nice billet down here. Trouble is, our public relations people aren't a patch on the reps for the Heavenly Host. Given us a really black name, they have. All this eternal torment nonsense! Pitch-forks, flames and red-hot pincers—I mean to say! Throw enough mud and some always sticks, you see..."

"You mean—it isn't like that at all?"

"Course it isn't! Just think about it – who is actually allowed down here? Is it our enemies? No, squire—it's the ones who supported our chief! Why would he punish the very people who proved themselves to be on his side? Now, if an angel somehow got down here, it might well get its feathers a bit ruffled—know what I mean?" This time he positively guffawed. "But life down here is pretty cushy for the inmates, all things considered. Especially if you were a serial killer or a rogue banker—plenty of kudos there... Why—even lowly forgers and petty criminals are well respected.

You should just see the accommodation! And the food! I tell you, it's a picnic down here. Always plenty going on—no risk of getting bored down here, boy. Laugh a minute, it is!"

I swallowed hard. "About this—lift, or whatever it is. I feel I should report to the Recording Angel as I was supposed to do. Get a second opinion."

He looked at me aghast. "I'm offering you the chance of a lifetime, Squire! Tell you what..." he winked and tapped the side of his nose "I could let you in straight away—no names, no pack-drill. Just sign this bit of paper and I'll let you in through that big door over in the corner. I've got a little phial of blood all ready to go. Group AB—Rhesus positive, aren't you?" He rummaged in the top drawer of his desk and selected a plastic sample bottle of bright red fluid. He waved it in front of me. "We really cook with gas down here you know (if you'll pardon the pun, Squire!). Neat little time-saver, this," he smirked, as he placed the phial on the desk, along with a quill pen.

Then he walked to the big oak door in the corner of the room, turned a massive golden handle and opened it slightly. The sound of riotous laughter came from within. However, it might have been pre-recorded canned laughter like they have on TV game shows—it's difficult to tell.

"If it's all the same to you, I think I'd like to have a word with the Recording Angel first. I may well come back later."

The demon shrugged. "They are real bureaucrats up there! Don't say I didn't give you fair warning..." He sniggered quietly to himself before pulling a lever at the side of his desk.

—ooOoo—

So here I am, stuck in limbo for eternity.

"Let me out! Can anyone hear me? Please, I'll agree to anything—but...

...let me out of here...!"

Double-Dealing

25th May 2023

Messers. Christobies' Auction House
London
F.A.O. Ms. K. Blount (Contemporary non-British Art)

Dear Ms. Blount,
    We have never met, although I have attended
many of Christobies' sales in recent years, both as vendor
and buyer. I am addressing this letter to you, as the objects I wish to dispose of are probably closer to your field
of expertise – "Contemporary non-British Art" – than
that of anyone else on the staff.
    In all, there are thirty-seven "objects" I wish to
sell. I enclose an image of each and dimensions are given
on the reverse. These were legitimately acquired by way
of trade, but in such astonishing circumstances that I am
reluctant to put anything in writing at this stage.
    Despite the indifferent quality of the photographs,
I feel sure that they will give you some indication of the
unusual, indeed unique nature of these artefacts, and
their high aesthetic merit.
    I would be most grateful if you, or one of your
staff, will contact me with a view to examining these
items in the near future.
        Yours sincerely,

        Randolf Bellamy.
        Sevenoaks, Kent.

(Discretion is the better part of Valour!)

Routing: Christobies' Internal E-Mail Server

Date: 27 May 2023, 10:13 a.m.
From: K. Blount <K.Blount@mcah.com>
To: Charles Penrose <Director@mcah.com>
Subject: Mr. Randolf Bellamy of Sevenoaks, Kent

Mr. Penrose,

I enclose a curious letter from the above, together with the images he mentions. Have we any knowledge of him? Is he a crank? The objects are most peculiar; very diverse and extremely intriguing. I am tempted to arrange a visit-- I'd rather like to see these items for myself. What do you think?

Kate

Katherine Blount, Curator
Contemporary Non-British Art
Messers. Christobies' Auction House
London, UK
www.mcah.com

Routing: Christobies' Internal E-Mail Server

Date: 28 May 2023, 2:52 p.m.
From: Charles Penrose <Director@mcah.com>
To: K. Blount <K.Blount@mcah.com>
Re: Subject: Mr. Randolf Bellamy of Sevenoaks, Kent

It is an odd letter, with still odder pictures, but our records suggest that he is perfectly above-board. We have had dealings with him, but in the past he seems to have specialised in English furniture and 18th & 19th C. British and Continental paintings.

By all means arrange to go and see him. To be on the safe side, take Geoff Manders along. He can take some better pictures for us, but more to the point, he will provide some, well, some security for you if Bellamy turns out to be as odd as his letter might suggest.

Charles Penrose, Director
Messers. Christobies' Auction House
London, UK
www.mcah.com

Routing: Christobies' Internal E-Mail Server

Date: 7 June 2023, 2:37 p.m.
From: K. Blount <K.Blount@mcah.com>
To: Charles Penrose <Director@mcah.com>
Subject: Visit with Mr. Randolf Bellamy

Mr. Penrose,

Geoff and I went to see Mr. Bellamy and his "objects"
yesterday. In my opinion he's as mad as a hatter!
However, the objects are truly astounding - I've never
seen anything remotely like them before.

If we do take this on, and frankly I don't see how we can
risk not doing so, it could be the biggest coup we've had in
a very long time. It will need stage-managing on a grand
scale. Vast publicity, expensive catalogue, lots of hype.

The thing is, we daren't say anything about source
or provenance, as you will realise when you read the
attached transcript of our meeting. (Fortunately I took
the precaution of wearing my wrist-recorder.) I have just
completed the transcription. You must read it!

Kate

Katherine Blount, Curator
Contemporary Non-British Art
Messers. Christobies' Auction House
London, UK
www.mcah.com

Messrs. Christobies' & Auction House
London

7 June 2023

**Edited transcript of digital recording
dated 6th June; 1405hrs - 1627hrs.**

(Speaker - Randolf Bellamy unless otherwise stated.)

.....What we'll do then, is go round to the barn and let you have a look at the stuff first. Yes, you can take photographs... then we'll come back to the house and discuss it over a cup of coffee. Or something stronger if you like - you might need it!.... *(The next twenty minutes omitted; consists largely of gasps of astonishment.)*

....Right then, coffee for you it is, Miss Blount, and a whisky for you, Geoff. Think I'll join you....*(Kitchen sounds and the clink of glasses).*

Now, I suppose you are going to ask me where this lot came from, and the name of the artist. Well, I'll tell you, but you aren't going to believe it; I know I wouldn't! Anyway, please don't interrupt; I'll tell you what happened and you can ask questions afterwards. This is the absolute truth, as God is my witness!

About three weeks ago I was up in Cumbria, meeting some dealers and looking round a few salerooms. Some nice stuff. Surprised me, I can tell you. I bought a few bits and bobs -- I was in the Landrover, so I couldn't take anything big. One day I was out in the wilds not far from Penrith and I came to this pub in a village - pretty little place, Eamont Bridge it's called. I was feeling a bit peckish and saw that they did bar-meals, so I turned into the car park, locked up and went in. I ordered a meal and while I was waiting, I looked up at the false ceiling beams, which were absolutely festooned with jugs of all shapes and sizes. Dozens and dozens of them, including a few very nice old ones which would be worth a bob or two in the trade.

Anyway, I had my meal and half a Mild, and was just about to leave when I saw this "thing" hung up with nylon cord above the door. It was about the size and shape of a rugger ball. No, a bit bigger. But it sort of shimmered in the light, something like fish-scales. It had lots of tiny serrated ridges running from end to end; felt sort of rough when you ran your fingers across them.

"What the devil is that?" I asked the barman.

"Fossilised bath-sponge," he said with a straight face. Right joker, that one. Anyway, to cut a long story short, he told me the landlord had bought it from an old chap in the village, who'd found it in his garden one morning a couple of weeks earlier. Wasn't there the night before - just appeared from no-where. Well, the local paper ran a little piece about it, with a picture."

The barman showed me the cutting. Various theories were

2

put forward, but nobody had the remotest idea what the thing could be. Some idiot suggested cutting it open with a hacksaw. In fact the tried, but luckily the blade wouldn't touch it! The landlord came to the rescue and bought it.

"Twenty-five quid he paid old Charlie for it and it's been hanging up there ever since," the barman said.

Well, I asked to see this landlord. I wanted the thing, whatever it was. We haggled for a bit, but eventually I got it off him for fifty.

Next day I came home. It was a long journey, so I unloaded the Landrover into the barn and put the queer object into my workshop at the end. Next day I started to examine it with that big illuminated magnifier you saw clamped to the workbench. I use it for delicate restoration work. Well, the mystery object was surprisingly heavy. I picked it up and shook it gently. It didn't rattle. I had no idea what it was made of - not metal or glass, or any sort of plastic. I did a few tests.

(*Voice of Kate Blount*) Could we possibly have a look at it, Mr. Bellamy? You didn't show it to us ....

(*Bellamy*) As a matter of fact, I can't. I'll come to that in a minute, just bear with me.

I couldn't make top or tail of it. Examined it inch by inch. Eventually I discovered a tiny hole, no bigger than a pin-prick exactly at one end. I thought about it for a bit, then

3

decided to have a poke around. I got a very fine needle and pushed it in, very slowly and gently, until it met a resistance.

I was leaning forward in my chair, watching carefully through the bench lens, and as I withdrew the needle a puff of dust, or some sort of gas, came out. Immediately I felt all my body go stiff. There was no pain, but it was just as if I had been turned to stone. My eyes could move and focus, and I could breathe, but that was about it. Whether I wanted to or not, I was forced to watch the weird things that followed. I was sitting at the bench, looking through the lens, remember.

First, the thing elongated, becoming more zeppelin-shaped. Then it rolled just a bit before a whole segment of one side hinged out and down to rest on the bench. Then came the most incredible part of all! About two dozen minute creatures came out. Without the magnifier I would probably have thought they were ants or something, but quite clearly they weren't. Some of them had wings - artificial, I think, and they soon flew off out of my field of view. The others started exploring around the top of the bench, while I just sat there, feeling a bit like Gulliver must have done when he was tied down by the Lilliputians...

(*Geoff Manders*) How many legs did they have?

(*Bellamy*) Blessed if I know! They didn't have legs like insects. They were long squiggly things - more like snakes, or the arms of an octopus. And the number

4

seemed to vary. Anyway, as I was saying, one of them
was a bit taller than all the others, and he was wearing a
complicated sort of silver helmet with little spikes and
tubes all over it. He was probably their leader. I'm sure he
- or she - was the one who spoke to me....

(*Geoff Manders; tone of incredulity...*) Spoke to you! It
spoke! This whisky is very good, Mr. Bellamy, but I don't
think I should risk another...

(*Bellamy, angrily*) Look here, young man - if you're
implying what I think you are, you can clear off, the pair
of you. I said you wouldn't believe me, but I didn't expect
to be accused of...

(*Kate Blount, hastily*) Geoff. didn't mean it like that, Mr.
Bellamy! It's just that - on the face of it - your story is ...
well, we couldn't very well put anything about this in the
catalogue ...

(*Bellamy*) Catalogue be damned! I'm just telling you
what happened. If you're not prepared to listen, without
interruption, you can get out right now and I'll contact
one of the American or Chinese auction houses.
Now, where was I ? Ah, yes ... This leader, or interpreter,
whatever he was, spoke to me. But not speech as we
know it. A kind of telepathy. I was in some sort of trance,
remember, and I heard this voice inside my head. It was
my own voice, as a matter of fact, but I certainly couldn't
have been speaking out loud.

Now we are coming to the really interesting bit, because

5

what he told me was this - they are dealers in antiques and objects d'art from other worlds! Big demand for exotic goods on their planet. Back there, of course, no-one could tell whether the stuff they took back was good, bad or indifferent, of its kind, but they are conscientious traders who only deal with bona-fide dealers and always give the provenance of everything they purchase.

No! don't you dare interrupt...

Purchase, I said. Not in currency, but in kind. Good old-fashioned barter. They had already taken a look round my barn, which was pretty well stocked with some good furniture and paintings. They were genuinely interested and said they wanted to take a lot of my stuff. Well, I wasn't in any position to argue, but they said they'd play fair and let me take my pick of their own goods. At that point I would have thrown a bit of a tantrum if I'd been able - what on earth would have been the good of a collection of alien objects you'd need a microscope to examine? Would they be sending round a space-pantechnicon next day to collect my stuff? What would the neighbours say when it arrived?

Well, they didn't seem to understand sarcasm. The leader-fellah explained; it's just a matter of getting the right scale.

Apparently they nearly always have to do a bit of adjustment, but very rarely as much as this. My stuff they would shrink down to a suitable size and take it into their ship. Whatever I chose from theirs, they would

6

expand by the same factor. Just then, two of the fliers returned. They had a net with something inside it. They lowered it very gently onto the bench in front of the space-ship before they landed.

Inside the net was an absolutely perfect miniature version of a girandole mirror I got at a sale in Ipswich a few months ago. After they had loaded it carefully into the ship they flew off for more. The translator asked me all about it, and from what I could see, he made some notes on a little pad. Then some more fliers arrived with more loot from my stock, all reduced to about a twentieth of its real size. Backwards and forwards they went; my stock was getting a bit low! The last to arrive were four fliers carrying a complicated-looking machine with a ridged tube like the hose of a vacuum-cleaner at one end. The interpreter explained that this was a "Variable-scale Induction Module" which had reduced the best part of my stock to its present dimensions. I was amused to see they'd included some cans of white emulsion paint I was going to put on the walls of the barn; you should have heard the tale I told them about the stuff - by the time I'd finished they thought it was the best thing they'd found!

When everything had been safely stowed, they started to unload their own trade-goods. Amazing stuff, as you have seen. It was by far the most difficult deal I've ever struck, because I had to make snap judgements on the products of a totally alien culture. For all I know, it might be pure junk - you know - glass beads for the natives. But I don't think it is. For some reason I trust those strange little creatures. I went mainly for what they said were representational paintings - but just what they are meant to represent I haven't the foggiest idea.

The problem is, he wrote out a card for every piece, attached it to them, so that the cards were enlarged at the same time. Well, like a fool, I didn't think to remind him to write it in English. So, every item has a full provenance and description in their native script, which consists of clusters of dots and a few wiggly lines. Absolutely useless! Well, I took a chance on some interesting sculptures and furniture -- but it's difficult to know which is which.

Well, we haggled for quite some time, and I've no idea whether I've been swindled or made the deal of a lifetime. Eventually they lined up all the items we'd agreed on, thirty-seven of them, and he told me he was going to unfreeze me. He had this little gun-thing and pointed it at me. "I'll freeze you again if you make any unexpected move," he warned. Another puff of gas appeared and instantly feeling flooded back into me. It was a bit painful at first, but I could move. I moved very cautiously...

Two of the fliers took one of the sculptures down to the floor and the operators of the variable-scale what-not pointed the flared nozzle of the tube at it. It went a bit blurry, then suddenly there it was, twenty times bigger, and I got my first proper look at a piece of alien art. It's that piece standing on its own in the workshop, by the way; too damned heavy to shift out of there. In fact, I thought it was just a shade too big, so I got them to

8

reduce it just a touch until I was satisfied. Then they took all the rest into the barn and enlarge it by the same amount - about sixteen or seventeen times, I reckon.

Well, the deal was done. My weird visitors climbed back into their ship and the ramp closed behind them. It changed shape again, becoming long and slender like an artillery shell. Amazing! It simply ignored the laws of gravity, rising up until it stood on its flat end. Then there was a blinding flash and the thing vanished, leaving a neat hole punched right through the roof of my workshop. I was just...

(Transcript ends, the recording disc being fully used)

Routing: Christobies' Internal E-Mail Server

Date: 7 June 2023, 4:14 p.m.
From: Charles Penrose <Director@mcah.com>
To: K. Blount <K.Blount@mcah.com>
Re: Subject: Visit with Mr. Randolf Bellamy

Kate,

Thank you for your last e-mail, transcript and Geoff's photographs. As you say, our Mr. Bellamy seems to be a certifiable lunatic, but if these items turn out to be his own work, which seems the most likely scenario, he may also be a genius. You are certainly better able to judge this than I, but the more I look at Geoff's photographs of the things, the more impressed I am. They really are astonishingly original and the craftsmanship is superb.

Surely Bellamy must see that, even if he believes it himself, no-one else is going to accept this codswallop! Do you think you can persuade him to put these works into a special sale under his own name? Humour him a bit. I'm sure it would make him very rich and famous overnight, and it would make our Shareholders very happy.

By the way, strictly speaking, this sale should be handled by Sidney Wallsham, as Head of Contemporary British Art. I've already had a quiet word with him and he's happy enough to leave everything to you in the circumstances. I showed him the pics, which made him sit up a bit, but after he'd read the tape transcript he didn't seem any too keen. I don't think he wants to tangle with our Mr. Bellamy! I take it that you are willing? It will be quite a feather in your cap as far as the Board is concerned.

If you require assistance of any kind, feel free to contact me at any reasonable time. I do not intend to raise this matter at the monthly staff conference next week. We will announce it as fait accompli at the July meeting. I've squared this with the Board, obviously, and they back us to the hilt.

Charles Penrose, Director
Messers. Christobies' Auction House
London, UK
www.mcah.com

Routing: Christobies' Internal E-Mail Server

Date: 8 June 2023, 10:22 a.m.
From: K. Blount <K.Blount@mcah.com>
To: Charles Penrose <Director@mcah.com>
Re: Re: Subject: Visit with Mr. Randolf Bellamy

Mr. Penrose,

I am grateful for your confidence and your backing. I have set things in motion.

Bellamy agrees, reluctantly, to claim all the works as his own. He was art-trained and is a skilful restorer, so I think we can pull it off; he has the right background.

We've started preparing the catalogue and Geoff spent two days with Bellamy taking top-quality shots for it - lights, drapes, the lot. You'll like them, I promise. There's one snag, by the way. Many of the materials he uses in the sculptures are very peculiar. Some awkward questions might be asked. Bellamy shrugged it off. "Trade secret" he said, tapping the side of his nose. I hope that will be enough to satisfy the curious, but I hope some chemist doesn't get too close to them.

I'm working towards 24th August for the date of the sale. Will that be OK? Our larger octagonal room is available then, and we need it to give a bit of "breathing space" for the exhibits. Most will be wall-hung and I've ordered plinths for the free-standing items, some of which are very heavy. We'll start transporting the pieces to our basement around the middle of next month if you agree on the date. We'll have to discuss insurance, of course, in the very near future.

Again, many thanks for your backing. I'm glad Sidney Waltham backed off – or should I say retired gracefully, leaving it to me! You know I'll do everything in my power to make a real blockbuster out of this – my reputation, such as it is – is at stake!

Kate

Katherine Blount, Curator
Contemporary Non-British Art
Messers. Christobies' Auction House
London, UK
www.mcah.com

Messrs. Christobies' C Auction House
London

DRAFT

17th July, 2023

PRESS RELEASE

Messrs. Christobies' Auction House

is proud to announce

An Exclusive Special Sale By Auction
of
Sculpture, paintings, and constructions
by
R. L. Bellamy, Esq., F.R.S.A.

To be held in the **Great Octagonal Room**
on **14 August.**

This as yet unrecognised artist is a man of quite exceptional talent and versatility. A collector of British and European paintings and furniture, he has shunned publicity for his own works. None of the truly sensational items in the sale have previously been exhibited to the public.

The sale comprises his life-time achievement and it is safe to say that this occasion represents a landmark in the field of contemporary art.

(continued on next page)

PRESS RELEASE (continued)

Sale to commence at: 10.30 - 12.30 hrs (lots 1-17),

Resuming at 14.00hrs and continuing until the last lot
(No. 37) is disposed of.

Fully illustrated catalogue available,
price 45 guineas inc. postage.

Caption for illustration, which we will supply:

LOT 11 - Construction No.4, 1998.
115cm. x 46cm. x 97cm.

Hardwood carving, with filigree metal
and coloured polymers.

Price guide £750,000 - £1.2M.

Sevenoaks, Kent.
19 August 2023

Miss K. Blount
Messers. Christobies' Auction House
London

Dear Kate,

(If I might be forgiven the liberty of addressing you in such a familiar manner, on such short acquaintance..)

I have just returned from the octagonal room, where I witnessed the last of my works being hoisted onto their plinths. I say "my" works in the sense of being the owner of these wonderful objects. However, I am actually beginning to feel that I really am their creator after having lived with them for many months, and having so often rehearsed the scripts which you prepared with such skill for the media.

I appreciate that the suggested "guide prices" shown in the catalogue are purely conjectural, but if they realise only a quarter of your estimates, I will become a multimillionaire overnight! It's good to know that so many international galleries and private collectors are to be represented at the sale.

My most sincere congratulations on the arrangements you have made. I was informed that you had left the gallery shortly before my arrival; I'm so sorry to have missed you on this occasion.

I look forward to meeting you again, about an hour before the start of the sale. Perhaps afterwards you would do me the honour of dining with me at an establishment of your choice, before we go on to take in a show, perhaps? Afterwards, well, who knows? Your acquiescence would complete the happiness of a lonely (but by then <u>extremely wealthy</u>) old man.

In all sincerity,
Your most grateful admirer,
And ever your <u>obedient</u> servant,

Randolf

Routing: Christobies' Internal E-Mail Server

Date: 20 August 2023, 9:16 a.m.
From: Margaret <Exec_Secretary@mcah.com>
To: Charles Penrose <Director@mcah.com>
Subject: URGENT! Voice Message from K. Blount

Mr. Penrose, I believe you will want to see this message
from Ms. Blount right away. I have transcribed her voice
message below:

Margaret

M. Daniels, Executive Secretary
Messers. Christobies' Auction House
London, UK
www.mcah.com

Voice message recorded 20th August 2023, 0417 hrs
on Director's phone line:

Mr. Penrose, this is Kate speaking. I don't know how I can
possibly break this news to you!

About an hour ago our night-security staff telephone me,
reporting that the Bellamy collection had been stolen. The
entire collection!

It took less than half an hour for me to dress and drive to the
saleroom, and on the way there I was praying that this was
some ghastly practical joke being played on me. I arrived to
find the place alive with security people and policemen. All
the lights were on and men were examining every door-lock
and window-fastener. It was true, Mr. Penrose -- everything
has gone! Even that massive two-ton statue!

The senior security man, Mr. Elders, took me into his office and gave me a strong black coffee with brandy in it. Then he opened the lid of his desk and pointed inside. "I collected these from the gallery as soon as the discovery was made. I've not shown them to anyone else as yet. It's some sick sort of joke, I suppose," he said.

Inside the desk were thirty-seven miniature replicas of the Bellamy items, perfect in every detail.

Mr. Penrose, I think Mr. Bellamy must have been telling the truth all along! Something must have happened to the "variable-scale induction" thing aboard the ship. Somewhere in space, a collection of paintings and furniture from Earth must have suddenly gone back to their original size inside a space-ship less than two feet long. This is frightful! Think of those poor little creatures dying like that, and our sale ...

You will find my letter of resignation waiting on your desk; I thought it best to write it out now. I'm sure the Board will demand it.

I don't know how you are going to break the news to Mr. Bellamy. For personal reasons I could never be persuaded to see or speak to him again.

Worst of all, I simply cannot imagine what our insurers are going to say about all this...

< Recording Ends >

Bandy and the Fort Knox Carpet

Private and Confidential.
F.A.O. Mr. J.K. Corlett, Solicitor.

Dear Sir,

As God is my witness, I am innocent!

Just go down to the Tanners' Arms any night and ask them about old Joe Andrews –

"Joe? Never! Wouldn't hurt a fly, not him!" That's what they'll tell you. Just ask any of them. All right, so I do have a bit of "form". Done a bit of porridge. Twice. I admit it - but never any violence. Petty criminal, that's me. But murder – I ask you!

It started about half ten one morning about two months ago, when there was this tap-tapping on the door. The bell doesn't work; been meaning to fix it, but I never got round to it, somehow. Too late now, anyway...

Well, I opened the door and there was this funny little guy standing there shivering. He was about five-foot nothing in his socks. Well, sandals, I should say. He was wearing a scruffy old Macintosh, with the edge of some sort of cream-coloured robe hanging out below it. He'd got weedy, bow legs without a trace of hair on them. Shaved them, for all I know. His head was covered with a black fur hat a bit like a sawn-off busby. It was far too big for him and rested on his ears. In one hand he held a great big canvas grip. He looked a real sight, and I almost started laughing until I looked closely at his face. He had high cheekbones - you know, sort of Slavic - and a small droopy moustache, and dark, sad eyes like a spaniel. His skin was a yellow-green, like somebody with Jaundice under a cabbage-coloured spotlight. It was the saddest face I had ever seen, and I didn't feel like laughing any more.

"Well," I said, looking him up and down.

He looked furtively along the street before replying. "Honoured Sir, might it be that the room you are offer for lettings, available still might be?" He pointed a finger at the notice my dear wife had replaced in the window a few days earlier. She'd had to tear off the bottom bit "NO COLOUREDS" after that bit of bother with the Race Relations people.

I didn't like the idea of taking him in as a lodger. What would the neighbours say?

To hell with the neighbours, I decided: we needed the money! But, did he have the money - it certainly didn't look like it.

I was still wondering whether I should tell him we'd just rented it out to somebody else and send him packing - when he smiled! It was a lengthy business. First his soft, sad eyes began to light up, then the smile began. It started surface-thin, like a drop of oil on water, spreading and changing, then it got somehow "deeper", until those dark eyes of his twinkled from the bottom of a pair of wrinkled pits. It must have been a long time since the little man had smiled – as if he'd almost forgotten how to do it. But when it was complete, it was a thing of beauty. And it was infectious; I found myself suddenly grinning as I motioned him into the hall.

I told him the terms, adding a couple of quid a week to be on the safe side; I could always come down a bit if necessary. Not that I expected him to accept; I wouldn't, anyway - not on your life!

His smile slowly vanished as he did a bit of mental arithmetic, then flickered on again. "That most acceptable, will be, Mr...?"

"Andrews. Joe Andrews to my friends," I responded, then wondered why I had said it.

"An-dar-rew-ez," he repeated slowly and carefully, nodding as he pronounced each syllable.

I'm usually pretty good on accents, but this one had me beat. It was like nothing I'd ever heard before. Understandably, as things turned out...

"But you haven't seen the room yet," I said, preparing to drop the price a pound or so when he got in there. It was a small bed-sitter, with a gas-stove on one side of the bricked-up chimney-breast and a washbasin on the other. There was a bed of sorts, an ex-army wardrobe and a single-bar electric fire. Ideal for a student, as we used to say. Nothing very special, you understand, but clean and respectable, although I'd be the first to admit that the carpet had seen better days. Anyway, as we went up the stairs, I asked his name.

"M'Bandalanavsky," he said.

"Come again?"

"M'Bandalanavsky..." His voice trailed off.

"Well, Mr... – here we are."

I paused and unlocked the door, and he followed me in, and stood there, just looking for a moment without saying a word. Then he went over to the window and looked out. I never claimed the room had a view, but it did - a derelict builder's yard, all overgrown with willow herb and bindweed. No one had ever showed much enthusiasm for the vista, but he rubbed his hands with satisfaction before examining the thick purple drapes at the window. He closed them, and opened them again before doing that smile of his. Next he examined the wallpaper, apparently fascinated by the faded pattern of roses all over it. A corner had peeled up a bit by the washbasin, he lifted it and examined it very carefully, poking the wall with his finger. Apparently he was reassured by the presence of distempered plaster beneath. He stroked the overlapping seams, his short-sighted eyes a few inches from the paper. Satisfied, he nodded, beaming at me.

"I think you will be comfortable here," I said, prodding the mattress with splayed fingers, "Mr. er... Bandanaversky," I added, proud at having remembered his outlandish name.

"M'Bandalanavsky," he corrected with an apologetic shrug, watching me turn back the bed-cover. "But that, Mr. Andarew-ez, necessary will not be." I thought nothing of the remark at the time. After all, he looked as if he were used to sleeping on far worse beds that this, or indeed on no bed at all.

Whilst explaining the details of the plumbing, the electric and gas meters and the stove, I took a closer look at him. He had removed his hat, to reveal a mop of frizzy black hair. His features, his peculiar accent and speech-patterns, his clothes, even his name, seemed to be an odd mixture of different racial elements. Where on earth can he be from, I wondered. His hands and feet, now that I saw them properly, seemed to be disproportionately large for such a tiny body.

I was just about to raise the business of a deposit, when he lifted the grip onto the bed, pulled back the zip and delved inside. To my astonishment, he produced a great double-handful of one pound coins and poured then onto the bedspread. He counted out more than three weeks-worth of rent before diving in again for more. He paid for four weeks in advance, and I stuffed the coins gratefully into my pockets. Before leaving him to settle in, however, I noticed that he made a very careful examination of the door and its lock. Its mechanism seemed to fascinate him, and he tried the key several times from both sides before crouching down outside and peering through the keyhole.

"Gadniviv... that is, thankings many, Mr. Andarew-ez," he said as I started downstairs. He'd said nothing about wanting a receipt, and I didn't want to bother him about rent-books and so on at such a time. He probably didn't understand, and he'd be very upset if he had to admit that he couldn't read or write. I can be a very considerate landlord.

I had accepted the coins without hesitation, but once downstairs I began to have misgivings; what if they were counterfeit? The only person I knew who could tell me for sure was Jimmy Hewitt, but he, unlike much of his output, was currently out of circulation. So I went to the bank and paid in most of Bandy's coins. The girl at the counter barely glanced at them as she set them against our joint overdraft.

Eva gave me the rough edge of her tongue when she returned from work to learn that I had let the room to some peculiar foreigner in sandals. She mellowed considerably when I tossed a small heap of the remaining coins on the table and placed the bank slip in front of her to prove he'd paid a month in advance.

The trouble began next morning when Eva came downstairs, curlers bristling. "What have you put down that toilet?" she demanded by way of greeting.

"What toilet?" I asked, like a fool.

"Since when have we had more than one lavatory in this house?" she demanded venomously.

"What do you mean, dear? I haven't put anything down it.

What is it, then? Disinfectant or something, do you mean?"

"I do not! If it wasn't you, it must have been that Mr. Ban... whatever..."

"M'Bandalanavsky," I prompted.

"All right, Bandal-whatsit, then. He must have done it."

"Done what, my dear?"

"Just come and see for yourself," she instructed, giving me one of her withering looks.

I realised something was amiss the moment I entered the bathroom; there was a most peculiar smell. Not unpleasant, just strange. The sort of smell brass might give off if it had a smell. Inorganic. Polished. Geometrical. I can't explain it - how can I describe an odour which is utterly unlike anything in my experience? It was neither attractive nor unpleasant; it didn't sting, it didn't take your breath away. It simply *was*. Much the same could be said of the bright turquoise, viscous-looking stuff which filled the lavatory pan almost to the rim, in defiance of all the known laws of plumbing. Bubbles were rising to its surface, popping faintly in the silence.

"Well?" Eva demanded, crossing her ample arms, with those knobbly elbows sticking out like a couple of walnuts.

"Er,... I don't know...er'..." I stammered in confusion.

"As I expected! You don't know. But I've a pretty good idea. It's that M'Bandal..."

"...anavsky," I said helpfully.

"Whatever. It must be him. He's not housetrained. I suppose we should just be grateful he didn't use the washbasin, or the bath. Well, you're the man of the house, in a manner of speaking, so it's your place to explain that civilised people flush the loo after they've used it." So saying, she grasped the chain.

"Don't!" I yelled in panic.

But it was too late. I watched in horror as the green froth rose to the very lip, heaved then thankfully subsided with a gurgling death rattle. To our amazement, the old, discoloured, crazed pan gleamed like new! Never, in the seventeen years we had lived in that house, had the lavatory been so spotless. Eva huffed and left the room.

Later, in the kitchen, she returned to the subject. "This Mr..." she raised a warning finger as I was about to supply the elusive name - "he must be a door-to-door salesman. You know, selling cleaning materials and so on. Well, that loo cleaner is pretty good stuff, I have to say that. Wonder what else he has?"

"I don't think he can be a salesman, dear," I ventured. He's only got that one grip with him, and that wouldn't hold much stock. In any case, he wouldn't be much good. Hardly speaks our language. Not proper, anyway. Sort of all mixed up and with a funny accent."

"Funny accent! And sandals!" she yelled, then clapped her hand firmly over her bosom, eyes bulging. She continued in a hoarse, frantic whisper. "You fool! Don't you see - Mr... Thing; he's a terrorist! You've rented our room to a fanatic who's making bombs in there! That stuff in the loo - he must have forgotten to flush it away!! Thank God I never went in there smoking!!!" Eva always tended to be a bit liberal with her exclamation marks when excited, but maybe she was onto something. A foreigner; secluded residential area; stacks of cash, paid in advance; no quibbles, no receipts asked for. That business with the lock on his door, the furtive glance over his shoulder before he entered the house. And now, strange chemicals in the lavatory. Yes, I thought, she could be right, at that.

Eva was all for getting the police in there and then. As she pointed out, there could be a reward out for this character. I thought again about his timid manner; and about that big bag of money. "Let's not be too hasty," I urged.

"What! Not be hasty when some foreign maniac is making bombs in your guest room?"

"Look, Eva, you've never even met him yet. He just isn't the type. He's probably a Buddhist or something - you know, the ones who won't kill a cockroach because it might be their grand-dad or something!"

"What rubbish you talk, Joe Andrews. Anyway, I want him out. Now."

"But Eva," I protested in desperation, the vision of heaps of coins fading before my eyes, "the Race Relations people would be on to us like a flash if we got rid of him without good reason."

"Without good reason! A fanatical terrorist using your own house as a bomb factory - isn't that good enough reason? What if he's a member of the I.R.A. in disguise?"

"Just one look at him and you'd know he is no Irishman. Leprechaun, perhaps, but I.R.A.–not on your life!"

"Whatever he is, I say he's got to go, Race Relations or not. Besides, they don't even know he's here. You didn't sign anything did you?" I shook my head, desperately trying to think of some way to reduce the burden of his heavily laden bag a little before he left the premises. Then I had an inspiration.

"Tell you what - if I climb into the loft and get above his room, there's a little hole in the plaster, right through that big ceiling rose. I could keep an eye on him, see what he's up to."

"And just how would you happen to know a thing like that?" she demanded, crossing her heavyweight wrestler's arms again. "I don't for one moment suppose you could have made that little discovery when that red-headed hussy had the room for a month before I found out her little game?" The glint in her eye could have cut plate glass. Fortunately I don't blush easily.

"Course not, Eva, whatever do you take me for? I'd completely forgotten about the hole until just then. I found it when we had to do that bit of re-wiring a couple of years ago. You remember, your Arthur helped me with it." The plate glass heaved a sigh of relief.

"Well, I'll see to it that you get a bit of plaster round it as soon as we're rid of this character. All right then, you get up there and keep an eye on him for a bit."

Thankfully, I left the kitchen and went upstairs. Access to the loft was through a trapdoor in the bathroom. I locked the door behind me, dragged out the ladder from behind the cistern and set it in place. I raised the loft cover and very quietly eased myself into the darkness above. I'd rigged up an old table-lamp when we'd been doing the wiring. I switched it on and it gave just enough light to be able to step safely from joist to joist above the lath and plaster ceilings. I'd also nailed a few planks around the middle of the guestroom during the all-too-brief time when "that red-headed hussy" had rented it. Many happy hours I had spent up there when Eva was at bingo...

Anyway, I lowered myself very carefully onto the old sleeping bag I had left on the boards and put my eye to the little hole. I'd drilled it up from the room below, placing it right in the middle of one of the plaster flowers in the big old-fashioned ceiling rose. From below it was almost invisible, especially as I'd replaced the sixty-watt bulb with a hundred. The glare helped to mask it, and it gave a perfect view of the centre of the room. A very interesting view at times, I can tell you!

It was a good thing I was lying down, or I might have toppled over in astonishment at the incredible scene below. Old Bandy had pushed the bed to the side of the room, and the thick curtains were closed. The light was on. His raincoat was hanging on the door, part of it hooked over the handle to cover the keyhole. These details I noticed later; for the moment I simply stared in disbelief at what was happening directly below. There, Bandy, in his cream robe was stretched full-length on a big mat. Not so astonishing, you might think, but the point is - the mat was floating in mid-air, about three feet off the floor!

I rubbed my eye and looked again, but true enough, there he was, fast asleep on this mat hovering above our carpet. It was brightly coloured, with lots of little spots, criss-crossed with bright green lines. He stirred in his sleep and as he moved, the rug swayed and rippled, adjusting itself to his new position. (How the red-head would have appreciated that!) No wonder he didn't seem bothered about the bed - he didn't need one.

He stirred again, now lying on his back and I realised he was about to awake. His eyes flicked open, but he quickly looked away, dazzled by the light. For a minute or so he stretched and yawned, then he climbed off the rug, fiddled with something underneath it, and with one finger, tapped three of the spots on the pattern. Instantly the thing floated down to the floor then rolled itself up. Bandy folded it neatly in half and stuffed it into his grip.

At this point I got up, and made my way, rather unsteadily, to the trapdoor. What I had just seen was impossible! As I was climbing down the ladder I heard a gentle tap on the door and someone tried the handle. "Half a jiffy," I shouted, my voice quavering a bit.

"Pardons, one thousands, Mr. Andarew-ez," came his reply and I heard him padding back to his room.

I went downstairs and poured myself a brown ale. I don't normally indulge so early in the day, but what I had seen had shaken me. Eva was out, probably gossiping somewhere. I settled down in my big armchair by the fire and thought things over. What I had believed I'd seen in that room was obviously impossible. Some trick of the light, perhaps. Trick...trick. That was the answer! Mr. M'Bandalanavsky must be a stage magician, the magic carpet one of his props. He must be performing at a theatre somewhere in the district. If I looked through the local paper I might see him advertised...

No mention of him in the Clarion. Nor in the "freebie" which landed on the mat a bit later. By that time I was going off the idea anyway. Perhaps it was some sort of hallucination. Couldn't be the D.T.'s - I like a glass or two, I admit, but not enough for that.

By the time Eva was back I still hadn't come up with any real idea of what was going on, but it didn't seem to pose any sort of threat to us. To stop Eva going off the rails again, I said I had seen nothing suspicious. To celebrate our extra bit of income, she had brought home a Chinese take-away, which saved me a job. I do most of the cooking, which I quite enjoy. Eva has this part-time job, which keeps her out mischief most afternoons. She used to work in a laundry, so when a couple of old biddies on Beech Road started making up-market aprons and fancy-dress stuff. (At least that's what they say it is, but I've got my own ideas about what it's used for.) Anyway, she got the job of ironing and packing them for the shops. The pay is fair and the arrangement places no extra burden on Her Majesty's overworked Inspector of Taxes. The point is, Eva is out most afternoons in the week, and being a man of leisure, I do most of the meals. Which led me to wonder how Bandy was getting on about food. He'd not been out for anything, and he can't have had much more in that mysterious bag of his, stuffed with coins and rugs.

Just as I was thinking that, I heard him coming downstairs. I had left the kitchen door open so I wouldn't miss him going out. He put his head round the door and smiled at me cheerfully. "Outings I am go, now, Mr. Andarew-ez," he said.

"Care to have dinner with us this evening?" I offered. "I'm doing steak and onions. Ready by six o'clock, will you be back by then?"

"Kindlings you are, thank you. Two hours I am back, but food already have. Other time maybe, thankings." He nodded sagely and gave a little bow as he left the room. My ploy had worked; I knew that he would be away for about two hours.

I waited until I heard the front door close behind him, then watched from the front-room window as he set off down the street. He was not carrying the grip, so I would get a chance to examine the magic carpet and whatever else was there. I locked the front door in case he arrived back earlier than he'd said, took the spare key to his room from the kitchen drawer and went upstairs.

The room was perfectly tidy, but there was a smell of cooking and I found that the gas-stove was on. Out of curiosity I opened it. Then I wished I hadn't. Trussed up in the baking tin was the dressed carcass of some small animal, which appeared to have six legs and a dark leathery skin. Around it were some peculiar vegetables, a bit like knobbly brown celery. I was very nearly sick at the sight of that weird creature. It must be something foreign, some sort of sea food perhaps. Did sea-cucumbers have legs, I wondered. There were some pretty nasty-looking things hanging up in the shop run by that Chinese family in Caister Street, but I'd never seen anything quite like this. I closed the door and was tempted to turn down the regulo a bit, but realised that would be a dead give-away if he noticed.

There on the floor, was the grip. I memorised its precise position before I lifted it onto the bed and unzipped it. There was the carpet! I took it out very carefully, surprised by its lightness, and unrolled it on the bed. It felt odd to the touch. I knew it wasn't a Turkish or Persian carpet or anything of that kind, which are thick and have a regular pattern. This was covered with lots of little coloured spots in no particular order, which were linked together by fine lines of bright green. It reminded me of something, but I couldn't bring it to mind. I touched one of the lines. It seemed to be woven from some sort of metal thread... Suddenly I had it! It was like some sort of complicated electronic circuit.

I tried to recall the sequence of three taps he had used to make it glide to the floor and roll itself up, but it was impossible - there were far too many spots to choose from. There were scores of them, all the same size, but in lots of different colours; who knew what might happen if I tapped the wrong ones? I turned my attention to the grip.

It was completely empty! Wise man; he had taken all the cash with him, or hidden it somewhere. Not that I would have touched a penny of it, of course. Goes without saying, I hope. I was merely curious.

Time was getting on, and I had much to do. First I replaced the hundred watt bulb with a one hundred and fifty. I was sure he would not notice any difference, and good lighting was essential for what I had in mind. I rolled up the carpet as neatly as possible, being very careful not to touch any of the spots, and put it away. I replaced the bag exactly where I had found it, then left the room, locking the door behind me.

Ten minutes later I was entering a certain electrical supplies shop in the neighbourhood. The owner owed me one or two favours for reasons which play no part in this story, and half an hour later I left carrying a package which was bulky but of no great weight.

Soon I was home again. Bandy was not waiting on the step and could not have got into the house without a key, so I locked the door behind me, knowing I still had the place to myself. I took the parcel up to the bathroom, then into the loft. I unpacked a very neat camcorder, which in normal circumstances would have been a very expensive bit of gear. I made a support for it from some wire and bits of strip-wood, and secured it in place with its zoom lens directly above the hole. It was a perfect fit. I loaded its little cassette and peering through the viewfinder, discovered I could see most of the room. It was only the carpet that really interested me, so I adjusted it to cover only the area directly below, and set the auto-focus. It was fitted with a remote control, which I could operate from the top of the ladder whenever I wanted. The packing materials I left in the loft. My preparations were complete. Of course, if Bandy happened to look up, directly into the light, it was possible he might see a glint of light reflected from the lens, but there was nothing I could do about it, I would just have to take the risk. The much greater threat to my plan was that he might turn the light off before I saw exactly how he operated the thing, and I did toy with the idea of re-wiring the wall-switch so that it was permanently on. That was something I could try later if necessary. Until then

I could only wait and hope.

My timing was perfect. A few minutes later I was in the kitchen getting our steak ready when the front door opened and in walked Bandy carrying three plastic bags. Seeing that I was busy he did not stop to speak, merely waving one of the bags at me as he made for the stairs. I gave him a minute or two to settle, then crept quietly up to the bathroom and switched on the camera.

Next morning I retrieved the cassette and fitted a new one. I had to wait until the afternoon when Eva had left until I was able to download the cassette onto a DVD then watch it on the computer. I was amazed how clear the picture was. What's more, the film was far more interesting than the usual junk they put on telly nowadays.

As it started, Bandy was unpacking stuff from his plastic shopping bags, and placing things on the bed, just outside my view, but I could see each item as he lifted it out. First came a huge assortment of different kinds of vegetables. How he'd got a greengrocer to agree to it, I don't know, but believe it or not, there was only one of each kind. Five different single potatoes, one carrot, half a dozen varieties of apples, one orange, one tangerine, one grapefruit, a tiny cluster of grapes and so on.

The second bag contained a range of tinned goods, one of each, and all of the smallest size obtainable; then a selection of baby-foods, of all things; assorted sweets and chocolate bars; several different brands of cigarettes, five sorts of cigars, boxes of matches, various coloured throw-away cigarette lighters. It was all very strange.

The last bag contained books, mainly paperbacks with lurid covers.

Rubbing those big hands of his together, he straightened up and walked "out of shot" towards the window. There was practically no sound of course, as the microphone was above the lath and plaster work, so I couldn't hear him draw the curtains, but it was obvious he did as the lighting changed a bit. Then he re-appeared, reached under the bed and slid out the grip. Crouching close to the screen, I watched closely as he took out the carpet and unrolled it on the floor. Reaching beneath, he appeared to search for something on the underside, and a movement of his arm seemed to suggest that he was turning an invisible knob to the left. Withdrawing his arm, he looked carefully at the surface and deliberately pressed three spots - blue, red, blue, in that order. The carpet slowly rose from the ground, swaying a bit, like a kite in a gentle breeze. Then it stabilised, floating about three feet from the floor. I fast-reversed the DVD and went through the sequence frame by frame. Apparently there must be some sort of master-switch on the underside of the carpet which I had not noticed when I had examined it. It seemed to be pretty well in the centre. Presumably this turned the thing on. Then the "blue-red-blue" code commanded it rise. I repeated the section at normal speed, which seemed to confirm my thoughts. Then I allowed it continue.

Bandy placed his little library of books in the centre of the carpet, which sagged a bit under the weight. He adjusted the position of two or three of the volumes so that they lay within a rectangle formed by the four outermost green threads. Satisfied, he reached underneath and again fiddled with the "master switch"before tapping a sequence of five different "keys". Immediately the books seemed to shimmer as if vibrating at high speed. They turned silver. Then they vanished! As they disappeared, the centre of the carpet rose as if relieved of their weight. I fast-reversed, and went through it very slowly, frame by frame. I concentrated as hard as possible on one particular book, which happened to be a copy of Muriel Spark's *The Comforters*. At first the edges of the book became blurred, taking on the appearance of silvery fur, whilst the cover picture, a girl leaning pensively in front of a typewriter, remained perfectly clear. Gradually the fuzzy edge spread inwards, obliterating more and more of the picture until the fur coalesced, transforming the book into a shallow rectangular block. Then it faded, the pattern of the carpet below emerging magically from the blank space like a photographic image appearing on the paper in the developing tray. The book was gone, along with the others. I stopped the DVD and thought hard before allowing it to continue.

Bandy heaped the tinned foods and jars of baby-food onto the carpet, again ensuring that everything lay within the green rectangle, and repeated exactly the same procedure. Within seconds everything became "furry", then vanished. Another load, this time sweets and cigarettes went the same way, and he started to load vegetables...

Could Bandy's magic carpet be some sort of disposal unit, I wondered. In which case, why had he bothered to buy the stuff in the first place? No, that obviously made no sort of sense. He had clearly chosen the items with a good deal of care, and for some definite purpose. Suddenly the solution dawned on me - the thing was a ... transporter ... no, what was the word? – a teleporter like they have on Star Trek. "Beam me up, Scotty," and off into space go carrots and cauliflowers, paperbacks and dog food; all priceless stuff on Jupiter, no doubt.

I stopped the DVD and thought for a bit. Perhaps there might be something in the idea, weird though it was, because it did offer some sort of explanation about our lodger. If it were true, then Mr. M'Bandalanavsky was an alien from outer space! No wonder I couldn't place his accent, or make a guess about where he was from. He was not from some obscure ethnic group, but a real alien masquerading as a human being. Hence the strange mixture of racial elements in his speech and his clothing; even his curious name. No matter where he went on Earth, he would be accepted as some sort of foreigner. It was a clever disguise, for any mistake he might make, a slip of the tongue or a social faux pas, would be put down to his obscure background. Posing as a universal foreigner would be far less difficult than attempting to pass himself off as a genuine Englishman, Turk or whatever.

It was at this point that a really nasty thought occurred to me; that repulsive carcass I'd seen cooking in his oven - that was probably alien, too. The teleporter must be a two-way device, allowing him to dial up his dinner from somewhere in space. Why he hadn't teleported a ready-cooked meal, I had no idea, unless his 'sampling' expedition to Earth might include first-hand experience of terrestrial cooking arrangements. Anyway, if his equivalent of a chicken or a rabbit looked as horrible as that, what must the *real* Bandy look like? How many heads, for example? The more I thought about it, the less I wanted to think about it.

I switched on the video again.

Once he had finished his teleportation session, he slid his hand under the carpet and worked the main switch, then leaned forward so that I was unable to see his next sequence of commands. After a few seconds a thing like a Balaclava helmet made from thick baking-foil materialised in front of him. He pulled it carefully over his head and as he did so a cluster of telescopic filaments sprouted from the top. Sitting there half-naked with this ridiculous object on his head, he looked absolutely absurd. He turned the master switch again, jabbed some more buttons, then climbed onto the carpet. He closed his eyes, and I could see his lips moving, but no sound as he jabbered away to himself. Little points of light were flashing around the tips of the filaments - obviously the helmet was some sort of communications device and he was reporting back to base, wherever that might be.

The conversation continued for some time, and I kept fast-forwarding in short bursts. At last Bandy finished his report or whatever he was doing, and started doing interesting things again. I'd almost decided what my next move would be - straight round to the Police Station. Not that I've any particular regard for our boys in blue, but in the circumstances, I saw it as my sacred duty as a citizen and as a coward, to let them know there was a Martian in our spare room. I'd insist on speaking to Detective Inspector Duggan, just for the pleasure of watching his face when I told him what was going on up there, and the change that would come over it when I showed him this video as proof. Besides, there might be a reward out for this joker. And, of course, the Sunday papers would pay good money for a story like this, complete with pictures.

As soon as I saw the next bit, I started to have second thoughts about turning him in. He "vanished" the helmet then went over to his raincoat, took out got a big handful of money and tipped it onto the magic carpet. All the low denomination stuff he took off like an angler throwing tiddlers back, then programmed the controls again. A blur began to form around the little heap of coins, then the blur grew bigger. The fuzziness cleared, and the pile was five or six times as big! The carpet sagged in the middle under its weight.

Shame on you, Joe Andrews, I thought to myself—what,

turn in an honoured guest to the tender mercies of the local constabulary? A man who hasn't done a bit of harm to anybody? What's more, a man – well, a being – who could do me a great deal of good. Just an hour with that magic carpet and the instruction manual I was about to compile, and I would be able to keep the wolf a respectful distance from my door for years to come. No fiddling about with small change for me. A good thick wad of ten pound notes would do very nicely for starters. Then it dawned on me - notes were no good. If the teleporter were duplicating things many times over, it would be a dead give-away. The Inspector Duggans of this world are very superstitious about two or more banknotes which happen to have the same number; always means bad luck for someone, they do say. And somehow word just might get around that old Joe Andrews might be able to help them with their enquiries once more. No, notes were definitely 'out'. That was why Bandy had that big heap of pound coins when he arrived; clever chap - correction, clever life form - this Bandy! Anyway, a couple of afternoons that's all it would take, so long as I mastered the combination. Quite like old times. This video was the key to it all; all I had to do now was to draw up my manual. After all, Bandy had paid for a month in advance, so there was no panic.

My plan was simple and foolproof. Next day I would get hold of a big sheet of tracing paper, and when Bandy went out I'd make an accurate drawing of the pattern on the carpet, full size, with all the spots in their proper colour. Then I'd plot out the sequence of commands for the duplication programme and practice with it. The day after that I would be able to pay off the mortgage, get the dry rot attended to - it had got worse in the last year or two - and book a decent holiday abroad. Within a week financial embarrassment would be a thing of the past, and with a bit of luck, by that time Bandy would be in some high-security guest-house being interrogated by the egg-heads. The carpet would be all mine! It was an attractive proposition. Then another happy thought struck me - Dollars, Lira, Yen - there was no limit. What about other negotiable commodities - pearls, diamonds, camcorders, DVD players? A couple of hours would probably be enough after all; and I had three or four hours most days for at least three weeks–Bandy had paid in advance...

Then my stomach lurched to my boots as I realised that my dream could vanish in a flash. Money meant nothing to Bandy! Our peculiar lodger could walk off with his magic carpet next morning without worrying about a bit of rent-money. Even now he could be packing his bag and preparing to move on. Frantically I skipped through the remainder of the DVD. Nothing of consequence seemed to happen and it ended with the unedifying spectacle of Bandy asleep on his Fort Knox carpet.

As soon as it finished I went upstairs. I listened for a moment by his door and was just about to take a peep through his keyhole when I heard the lavatory being flushed. I slipped into our bedroom and closed the door quietly. A few seconds later I heard the bathroom door creak open and the soft pad of Bandy's feet as he crossed the landing. I watched through the keyhole and caught a glimpse of him entering his room. He was fully dressed, even to the shabby raincoat. I waited there, terrified he might reappear carrying the grip and the magic carpet from my reach for ever. I had half-decided that if he was holding the bag when he came out there might have to be a little accident on the stairs. I mean, it's not as if he were a real human...

I breathed again when he came out without the bag and started going down the stairs. A couple of steps down he stumbled on the worn carpet and I hugged myself in anticipation. But he recovered his balance and shortly afterwards I heard the front door close behind him. There was no time to lose.

Five minutes later I was also on the street, heading in the opposite direction, towards an office supplies shop. I bought a roll of draughtsman's tracing paper - thick heavy stuff that is almost impossible to tear, a wallet of smudge-proof coloured felt-tip pens and ten large bulldog clips.

Within twenty minutes I was in Bandy's room, tracing out the intricate pattern of the carpet in pretty exact colours. It took well over an hour and my knees were aching long before I had finished. I unclipped the tracing paper, replaced the carpet in the bag and made sure everything was in its proper place before leaving. I had confirmed the existence of the master switch. It wasn't easy to see if you didn't know it was there. It was right in the centre. If you slid a fingernail under the edge and pulled down, it extended on a minute telescopic spindle. I made sure

I didn't turn it before I pushed it back. Until I was absolutely certain I had the correct command sequence, I had no intention of activating the thing; for all I knew it might contain a self-destruct mechanism that would trigger in the event of improper use. Its presence explained how Bandy could sleep on the thing without getting deluged with six-legged chickens every time he turned over. The master-switch had to be activated before every command sequence, so lying on it, rolling it up or even folding it would have no effect. I took my precious tracing downstairs and practised with it, following every move Bandy made on the video. Then I locked it away in my big roll-top desk.

Bandy did not come home until early evening. Eva had got back at her usual time and we'd had tea before settling down to watch television. Now if my wife has a fault, and I'd be the first to admit that she does, it's that she's inclined to be avaricious. And impulsive. Yes, avaricious, impulsive and aggressive; those are her main faults, but she has others, of course. That's why I decided that it would not be in her best interests to learn what I had really discovered about our lodger. Besides, I had this suspicion that lying on her back with her arms and legs drawn up she might just fit within the faint green rectangle on the carpet. An idle and unworthy thought, no doubt, but somehow I could not banish it from my mind. Anyway, when she enquired about our guest, I told her that he seemed to spend most of his time reading and meditating. "About what?" she demanded.

I stared at her in disbelief. She can be very obtuse at times. Another of her faults. "How the hell should I know what he meditates about, I'm not a mind-reader," I snapped. Thankfully she let it go at that because some soap opera was starting. That was when I heard Bandy coming in. I gave him a couple of minutes then scampered up to the bathroom to start the next recording; knowledge is power.

Eva was in the house all the next morning, washing and ironing. I kept out of her way as much as possible, longing to get at the new tape. Bandy went out at about quarter past ten and to my intense relief, he was not carrying the grip. At last Eva went off to work, slamming the door behind her, as is her custom. I locked it behind her, then got out my tracing and placed it on the floor in front of the computer.

The second DVD began in much the same way as the first. From two plastic bags he produced an impressive array of children's toys. The third contained masses of glossy brochures from a travel agency. All these items he proceeded to teleport - or disintegrate - via the carpet. I followed his commands on my tracing then copied them onto another sheet, just the buttons used, as a numbered sequence. He dispatched his goods in six separate lots, giving me ample opportunity to practice and to verify that the same code was used in each case. I had certainly mastered one code sequence, but this was relatively unimportant. What I had to confirm was the duplication or multiplication mode.

The next part of the video showed something new. He activated the carpet, pressed five different buttons and appeared to jabber something at it. Then he tapped two more spots and sat there cross-legged, waiting. Half a minute later a blur began to appear. It resolved itself into a brightly-polished golden cube, about ten inches across. He lifted from the carpet and placed it on a small tray then slit open the top with a penknife. Apparently he did not approve of the cooking facilities we had provided and had whistled up some sort of inter-galactic fast food service, for he began eating the contents with a long-handled spoon. I deduced that the verbal instructions he had given were his order to the chef. This suggested that he was in direct contact with his base, so I must be sure never to activate that particular sequence.

When he had finished his meal he placed his empty food parcel, together with the plastic bags, wrapping material and other rubbish onto the carpet and whisked them out of existence with a few quick stabs of his fingers. I went through that bit again and recorded the combination on another overlay chart. This I marked "Waste Disposal Mode?" Could be useful, I decided.

Annoyingly, he didn't appear to need any more cash, so he did not use the "Multiplication" sequence that night. In fact, the rest of the video was a waste of time. After I'd whisked through it, I replayed the first one and plotted out another overlay recording the code for multiplying coins. This I labeled "Midas" and determined to take my chance with it next day. Next day!

The next day, I realised, was Thursday - half-day closing for the local shops; Bandy's shopping spree would be cut short, leaving me very little time to experiment. It was too late to do much today, but I was desperate to test the thing as soon as possible. I locked the front door, leaving the key in the lock, then taking my "Midas" overlay, I let myself into Bandy's room.

It was an eerie experience unrolling the magic carpet, knowing that I was about to tamper with an absolutely unique piece of alien technology. As I unrolled my overlay, my blueprint, my Access Card, my winning lottery ticket, I reflected on the countless pitfalls that might yet rob me of my inheritance. Although I was confident that I had obtained Bandy's PIN number, there could be built-in safeguards - was it somehow programmed to respond only to Bandy's fingerprints? How hard must the keys be pressed? Were there spoken commands I had not been able to record? Worst of all, was there some sort of remote surveillance system back at base? Another disturbing possibility was that the carpet was indeed a sort of interplanetary cash dispenser, with a limit on the amount which could be withdrawn; was Bandy's credit good, and would he be advised of my withdrawal next time he reported back?

It was now or never! I slid my hand under the carpet, eased the switch from its recess and turned it carefully until I felt a slight resistance. That must be it. I checked my overlay and tapped in the basic code to make it hover. It responded! I was halfway there.

When I touched the master switch again I found that it had returned to its original position. I turned it again and referred to my "Midas" overlay; this was the acid test.

I placed five one-pound coins and some loose change in the middle of the carpet, took a deep breath and punched in the code. Instinctively I drew back and covered my face with an arm, but nothing untoward happened, and a few seconds later the heap of coins went blurred, just as the video had shown. Suddenly the hazy patch enlarged, and resolved itself into a nice big heap. I quickly re-set the master and pressed the code buttons...

A couple of minutes later I was scooping handfuls of coins into a big metal wastepaper bin. It was a hell of a struggle getting it into the loft, and when I counted it later, found I had earned myself a nice little profit of nearly eight hundred quid!

Bandy could be back at any moment, but I was determined to try one more experiment. I had my grand-dad's gold hunter watch, a splendid piece, with a chunky solid gold chain and a big agate fob. I placed it on the rug and tapped in "Midas". I did it a couple of times more and was soon the proud possessor of sixteen identical antique pocket watches, all ticking away in perfect unison.

After that little demonstration there was no way Bandy could be allowed to rob me of the fruits of my ingenuity and hard work. I was very tempted simply to pack the carpet into the grip and walk away forever, leaving him and Eva to work things out in their own way. That's probably what I should have done, but another little scheme was evolving in my mind. I packed everything away, locked Bandy's door behind me and hid the watches in the loft. The tracings and videos I locked in the desk. I only just made it. Bandy was back, loaded with shopping bags as usual, as I was going into the kitchen. We waved to each other and I watched his skinny little legs disappear as he climbed the stairs.

That evening Eva went to her usual Wednesday night Bingo session with some of her cronies, which allowed me to do another small but significant experiment. The videos had shown that Bandy seemed to do very little in his room. He didn't read, write letters, listen to the radio or anything. Once his daily supply of samples had been sent off to outer space and he'd had a meal, he simply floated about on his carpet and was usually asleep by eight-thirty. Perhaps Venusians, or whatever he was, need more sleep than humans. What I had to find out was how deeply he slept.

At nine o'clock I eased myself into the attic and made my way across the rafters to my viewing platform. Very carefully I removed the camcorder from the hole, waited a moment, then placed my eye to the little hole. True to form, the light was still on. As far as I could tell, he'd never turned it off since his arrival. But then, coins for the meter were no consideration. As I expected, he was fast asleep. I replaced the camera and left. Soon I was outside his door, listening intently for any sound of movement. Hearing none, I tapped softly on the door. There was no answer. Encouraged, I tried again, a bit louder. Then louder still, but still no response. I smiled to myself - our guest was indeed a sound sleeper. I peered through the keyhole. I was in luck - the key was not in place, so I inserted my own. Turning it gradually, I felt it engage the wards and began to ease them back. The bolt shot back with a clatter which in my state of tension sounded like an explosion, but which in reality cannot have been more than a faint click. I froze in a trembling sweat.

I waited for a few seconds, my ear pressed to one of the panels. Was he waiting, wide-awake, with some sort of death-ray pointing at the door? I was sorely tempted to creep away - to return to the loft and see what he was up to. Eventually I decided to take my chance. I grasped the handle and turned it smoothly until I knew the catch was free. Then I swung it open and stepped into the room, ready to apologise for my intrusion and tell him that I had just heard that the Water Board might be turning off the supply for an hour or so next day.

The alien, a pathetic little figure, lay on his left side, facing away from me, arms and legs drawn up tight to his body. I was delighted to see that he lay completely within the outer limits of the green transmission rectangle. I certainly hadn't intended putting my plan into operation so soon, but I might never get such a perfect opportunity again. It was so easy!

Reaching beneath the carpet, I activated the master switch, then rapidly stabbed out the "Disposal" command I had rehearsed over and over again on my template. As I did so, he turned his head towards me, his eyes flicking open. To my dying day I will never forget the look of horror that spread over his face. It was the last thing I saw of him. Like the smile on the face of the Cheshire Cat, it lingered in my mind's eye after his body had vanished into some other dimension.

It was at this moment of triumph, when I had disposed of our paying guest, and taken charge of his priceless carpet, that I experienced feelings of remorse. However, the feeling passed, and I consoled myself with the thought that I had become an unsung hero, ridding the world of a potential threat to its very existence; "Mr. M'Bandalanavsky" could well have been reconnoitring for some invasion from outer space. In the circumstances, possession of the Fort Knox Carpet was no more than a just reward for my valiant action. Even so, I felt rather bad about trundling the little chap into space by means of his own waste disposal unit. If he still existed somewhere out there in the cosmos, no doubt he would also be feeling bad about this turn of events. I could not imagine him merely shrugging off the incident with a rueful smile as he slopped about some Venusian swamp in his sandals and dhoti. No, I thought, if he's still alive out there, he's probably reverted to type - possibly a twin-headed, fire-breathing monster, gritting his fangs and vowing eternal vengeance against poor old Joe Andarew-ez of Clapham. He'd got to Earth before, what was to stop him returning? Possibly with a few of his buddies...

Getting rid of Bandy in this way had seemed a good idea at the time, but I was beginning to realise that my action had been a little hasty. I should have been content to accumulate a nice little fortune and let him go on his inscrutable way when he was ready. As it was, Bandy, with or without supporting cast, could be back at any time, in a very bitter frame of mind. What was I to do?

My mind raced. First I would use the carpet to make my fortune as quickly as possible, then destroy it to prevent any risk of his return by that means. Then I would leave the district, or better, the country, in case he obtained some other means of transport.

I looked at my watch. I had at least an hour and a half before Eva returned. I made a start at once, duplicating coins by the thousand, along with video cameras, CD and DVD players, more gold hunters and assorted jewellery. As I worked, my mind turned to thoughts of the Mediterranean and the bevy of nubile, sun-drenched beauties who would soon be pandering to my every whim - and I have my fair share of whims. They would help to console me for the absence of my poor dear wife. She would be well provided for, though; I would see to that before my departure in a few days time.

At length I was through for the evening. I'd had to lay lots of extra floorboards over the joists and it had been back-breaking work hauling my booty up the ladder into the loft. Never let it be said that Joe Andrews is afraid of a bit of hard work in a good cause!

Every hour Eva was out during the next four days I was fully occupied. I opened five new bank accounts at different places, hauled thousands of pounds-worth of coins to the Bureau de Change to get high-denomination coins of other currencies, bought masses of Travellers Cheques, a nice selection of gemstones and so on. When the loft was almost full, I realised that since Bandy was no longer in residence, I could use his room as well. This speeded up the process no end, and soon it too was bulging with my hard-earned booty.

It was time to call a halt, but when it came to the point I could not bring myself to destroy the goose that was laying golden eggs with such gusto. For the present I was a very wealthy man, but if I were to spend unwisely, as I had every intention of doing, I might well regret having dismembered this priceless work of art. In the end I reached a compromise. I bought a large metal box fitted with locks, and placed it on the floor in Bandy's room. I folded up the carpet, bound it round with thick wire, and locked it away. I estimated it would take another couple of weeks to convert all my goods into cash and pay it into my various bank accounts and buy the stocks and shares I had selected.

Happy days!

The disaster happened next day. I was paying in a modest £15,000 in Euros at the foreign counter of the branch just round the corner from our house when we heard this muffled crash outside. The cashier lost count and had to start again. It took quite a time.

I left the bank, whistling cheerfully, twenty minutes later. As I rounded the corner it looked like a scene from the blitz. A fire-engine, two police cars and an ambulance stood outside the wreckage of our house. Men in various shades of blue were swarming about amongst the rubble. The gable end wall had collapsed outwards, the roof slumped over it. Thousands of coins were scattered like confetti. Out of the wall protruded Bandy's bed, six inches deep in gold hunters. The boys in blue had cordoned off the area and were occupying themselves filling dustbin sacks with brand-new cameras and hi-fi equipment, whilst the firemen were rummaging about looking for bodies.

As I arrived, shocked, stunned and miserable, Inspector Duggan took me by the elbow and guided me into a panda car, muttering something in my ear. If only I'd had that dry-rot fixed, this terrible business would never have happened. The weight of all that money was the last straw.

Well, the rest you know. They found the strong-box, still locked. Inside it was the dead body of a tiny foreign-looking chap trussed up in galvanised wire, and wearing nothing else. Naturally the fuzz took a pretty dim view of the whole affair. I had a bad fall going down some steps in the police station, so it's not easy for me to speak at present. That's why I've written all this down for your personal attention.

Well, if you are going to be my defence lawyer, it's only right you should know the whole story, just as it happened. You will, of course, realise that it is absolutely vital to find those DVDs and my overlays. Otherwise my account of what happened is going to sound a bit thin in court...

Sincerely,

Joseph Andrews

ABOUT THE AUTHOR

"Schooldays are the happiest days of your life" – what rubbish!"

Harry Fancy was born in Stockport, Cheshire in 1937. Leaving school virtually innocent of academic qualifications, he embarked upon a career in horticulture–to wit–he became an apprentice gardener in a public park! Within a short time he was compelled to undertake his two-year stint of National Service in the Royal Tank Regiment at Catterick Camp in Yorkshire. On returning to Debdale Park, Manchester, he undertook an intensive two year,

Photo courtesy of the Whitehaven News.

extramural course in Scientific Horticulture at Manchester University. Success in this course secured him a place on a two-year full time course at the Royal Horticultural Society's garden at Wisley.

After gaining an Honours Diploma from Wisley, a career in horticulture seemed inevitable, but almost immediately he completely changed course, becoming general assistant to the Curator of Vernon Park Museum, Stockport. Then, after a two-year period as Senior Assistant at Luton Museum, Harry was appointed Curator of his old museum at Stockport. He remained in that post for seven years (1968-1975). He and his family then moved to the historic, yet almost forgotten town and port of Whitehaven, Cumbria. For the next 21 years he was Curator of the museum, which towards the end of his career, was rehoused in a purpose-designed building called "The Beacon". This overlooks the historic harbour, the scene of the last raid on the English mainland by an enemy power. This was an expedition commanded by "The Father of the American Navy" John Paul Jones, who had actually been trained as a seaman at Whitehaven. His first experience of the odious slave trade as third mate of the Whitehaven-built slave ship *King George*.

In 1985 Harry was instrumental in acquiring for the museum the Whitehaven Slavery Trade goblet, arguably the finest specimen of English enamelled glass in existence (being examined in the photo by the author). It was decorated by William Beilby (1740-1819) and is the "odd man out" in his series of "Royal" goblets, of which eight survive. All bear the meticulously painted Royal arms of George the Third. Seven feature the feathers of the Prince of Wales and were produced to commemorate the Christening of the young prince in 1763. The Whitehaven example is instead embellished with the painting of a sailing vessel with the legend "Success to the African Trade of Whitehaven". It was used to celebrate the maiden voyage of the *King George* and is probably the highlight of the museum collection. Whilst the museum was temporarily rehoused in the Civic Hall, inadequate security led to the goblet being stolen and held to ransom. Beilby's masterpiece was eventually recovered, thankfully undamaged.

Throughout his career, Harry was a compulsive writer, producing a considerable number of information sheets and booklets. In different years three of his more substantial works were entered in the "Lakeland Book of the Year" competition. One was Highly Commended, another was the runner-up for the Rollinson Prize and the other won the Barclay Prize in 1992. For his own amusement, he wrote and continues to write, short fictional stories–from which the thirteen tales in this compilation were selected.

Harry and his wife, Margaret, reside in Nether Kellet, a tiny village in north Lancashire, England, where they have lived since completing a five-year sojourn on the Isle of Man in 2002.

www.ingramcontent.com/pod-product-compliance
Lightning Source LLC
Chambersburg PA
CBHW070918130626
46555CB00001B/186